Jess & Jasper

CLUB DECADENT BOOK THREE

K.C. FORD

eBook ISBN: 978-1-0691328-0-2

Paperback ISBN: 978-1-0691328-4-0

Cover Design: Katherine Ferguson

Edits: Katherine Ferguson

Formatted with Atticus

About

This is Book Three in the Club Decadent Series. Each book focuses on a specific pairing and can be read as a standalone. However, the series is best enjoyed in order.

When Jasper finds his wife's 'Dear John' letter, he wants to chase after Jessica immediately. But she'd used her safeword, and as her Dom, he'd never cross such a boundary. So he waited. Life moved on, yet it felt like he remained frozen in time until his sister Joanna needed him to rescue the daughter she and her husband fought like hell to have.

Unbeknownst to them, their surrogate had given birth in a growing Warzone, and when Jasper reached the triage hospital in the tunnels beneath the city, he came face to face with his estranged wife, holding his niece in her arms.

Jasper has waited more than three years, and he'll be damned if he let his wife walk away again without the two of them talking, fighting, or fu...well...you get the idea. ;)

Preferably they'd do all three.

Authors Note

This story is a high-heat, M/F, second chance, married couple romance with a stern, cinnamon roll, Dom, who will do everything and anything for his fiercely independent wife. If that's all you need to know, skip on ahead. If you need more details, please refer to the list of content and tropes on the next page. Happy Reading!

This book is written in third person with dual POV. There is an Age Gap (FMC is 30, MMC is 40). Note: The setting of the real-life war in Ukraine plays a part in this fictional story. Endometriosis and fertility issues for the FMC. Detailed discussion of pregnancy loss by a secondary character (Chp.10). Surrogacy. Trypanophobia – the MMC has a fear of needles. Panic attack. There is a brief mention of domestic violence that happened to a secondary character off-page. Adult language and situations. Explicit sexual scenes between consenting adults, including elements of BDSM and Kink (there's a bit of knife play). Miscommunication (resolved early on). Surprise Pregnancy. Tattooed and pierced FMC. My Wife/My Husband vibes. Good girl praise. You're it for me/It's always been you vibes. He spoils her relentlessly. A little bit of degradation. Hand necklace. He braids her hair. Crawl to me vibes. A Beyoncé Partition scene. Found family. Pop culture references. Guaranteed HEA.

The Playlist

Music plays a big part in this author's and these characters lives. If you enjoy some great club bangers, love songs, songs to 'get it on' to, and dash of Canadian hits. This is the playlist for you. Enjoy!

<u>Club Decadent Series Playlist by K.C. Ford</u>

Contents

CHAPTER ONE

Jasper

Why do they call these things baby showers?

There are no babies or showers, just a bunch of adults eating tiny sandwiches off tiny plates, standing around talking to each other about their jobs and families.

Jasper sighed and swallowed a mouthful of the scotch Jonathan handed him when he first arrived. As the majority owner of an exclusive BDSM club, the conversation around 'what do you do for a living?' usually turned awkward fast.

Yet hiding in what used to be his parent's kitchen conjured memories Jasper didn't want. It wasn't the death of their parents he dwelled on. No, his mind replayed the first time he'd met his wife. Joanna's one attempt at matchmaking.

"Jas? I'm home, and I brought a friend."

Jasper dropped the financials he was reviewing and pushed away from his desk. Did Joanna bring a boyfriend home for Christmas?

Jasper strode down the hall toward the kitchen. He stopped mid-step when he heard the sweetest voice speak to his sister in an urgent whisper.

"What are you doing? I'm sure your brother doesn't want an unexpected holiday guest. I'll head to my mom's place. She left the fridge stocked, so we can do Christmas next week after she returns from taking care of my Grams in Florida."

"I don't care how well stocked your mom left the fridge. You're not spending Christmas alone, Jess."

Jess…. Jasper rolled the name over his tongue, finding its irony beginning with a J fitting and amusing. He needed to know what the owner of such a sweet and sultry voice looked like.

Jasper rounded the corner with all the confidence he possessed. "No one should spend Christmas alone…." His words trailed off the moment his gaze met hers.

Joanna squealed and hugged the taller woman. "I told you Jasper wouldn't mind." Joanna turned toward him, a knowing smirk on her face. "Oh, Jas?"

Jasper had the damndest time dragging his gaze away from Joanna's guest. When he did, she said, "This is my dormmate, Jessica Harris. Jess, this is my brother Jasper Jones."

Jasper sipped his drink and shut the door on those memories. He'd be anywhere else if the guests of honor weren't his sister, her husband Jonathan, and their daughter Sara-Jane.

Well, not anywhere.

Jasper would be at the club, buried in work, or making sure those around him were happy and loved while pretending the missing piece of his heart didn't matter.

"There you are. Though I'm not surprised to find you hiding in here."

Busted.

After all, Joanna knew him better than anyone else.

"I'm not hiding," he muttered behind his glass, then finished his drink.

"Then what do you call lurking in the shadows of the kitchen while everyone else is out there?" Joanna asked with her hands on her hips. She's such a little spitfire.

"Taste testing," he said, snagging a mini quiche off a serving tray. "Dang. Those are good."

Joanna pulled him aside, not allowing him to grab another. Of course, she's right. He is doing his best to avoid everyone, but.... "Please don't make me play the poop game," Jasper blurted.

Joanna stared at him with a blank expression. Then bent over and snorted with laughter. "Oh, my god, I can't," she gasped, clutching her stomach.

When she calmed enough to speak more than wheeze, she said, "You're hiding because of a game to guess what melted chocolate bar they smeared in a diaper? And here I assumed you're hiding to avoid telling my neighbor, Mrs. Bradbury, about your kinky fuckery club."

Jasper coughed. "Language, Joanna," he scolded like she was a wayward teen and not a woman of almost thirty. "But you may be onto something." He conceded.

"No one cares, and I always get a kick out of you telling new people."

"Figures. You'd find shocking someone with delicate sensibilities into speechlessness amusing."

Joanna dropped her voice to a conspiring whine. "She won't stop talking. I want her at a loss for words, at least for one minute. Please? It'll be fun for me." Joanna's expression grew wicked. "Besides, we aren't playing the poop game. We have something much more fun. It's kind of up your alley and expertise."

"What baby shower game can I possibly be an expert on?" Joanna went to the covered easel near the dining table and flipped it up, revealing dozens of women's faces with similar expressions. Jasper looked between her and the easel. "I don't get it."

Joanna sighed over the indignity of having to spell it out for him. "Is it Labor, or is it Porn?" she asked, waving her hand beneath the photos like she's Vanna-fucking-White flipping a letter on the Wheel. "Get it?"

"Oh, I get it, and you won't need me to shock Mrs. Bradbury into silence when this will do a fine job of getting her to faint on your living room floor. You're incorrigible, sister mine," Jasper said, using the endearment he called her since she was a rambunctious toddler.

"You love it, brother mine," Joanna said, bumping his shoulder with hers. With her petite frame, it's more like she bumped his elbow.

Joanna topped out at five-five in heels. Jasper didn't know where she came from in their gene pool. His mother reached almost six feet, his father a couple inches more, and it surprised no one when Jasper grew to six-four while Joanna became their petite enigma.

"The hospital sent a new photo," Joanna said, shifting the subject to why they'd all gathered for this party.

"Sweet. Give Uncle Jasper a hit of his precious angel." His sister shared every new photo she received of Sara-Jane with him, and he treasured them like prized gifts. Joanna pulled up the album on her phone and flipped it around for him.

"Isn't she beautiful? I can't believe she's two weeks old already."

Jasper stared at the picture of his niece. Her downy hair looked strawberry blonde, a few shades lighter than his and Joanna's, while her pouty mouth was an exact copy of his sister's. "Janie's perfect."

Joanna smacked him, and Jasper hissed, rubbing his arm. "Jasper Jones, don't you dare call Sara-Jane, Janie. The J names stop with us."

"But it's tradition, and look at her sweet face. She looks like a Janie."

"It's Sara-Jane. It honors the tradition in a new way, and kids won't make fun of her when she has to present her family tree at school, damn it."

Jasper gazed at the picture a little longer, then handed Joanna her phone. "She can be Sara or Sara-Jane at school. To Uncle Jasper, she's Janie."

"Ugh. After you and Jessica got together, I swore I'd never end up with a man whose name started with a J, and the reason I went on a date with Jon in the first place is that he told me his name was Tom, and you assholes, backed him up."

Joanna pursed her lips. "Lucky for my sweet husband, by the time I learned the truth, I'd fallen head-over-heels in love with the guy and forgave him after some proper penance."

Jasper chuckled, ignoring the sharp pain at the mention of Jessica's name. "You know he's perfect for you. It didn't matter what his name was."

Jonathan was part of Jasper's military squad, and on what turned out to be their last mission, while successful, several didn't escape unscathed. Jon suffered burns and now carried the scars from their enemy's counterattack.

It took many months of rehabilitation and therapy for him to recover. Afterward, Jon joined Elite Security, the firm Xander Ward, another team member.

Jonathan got a five percent stake in the club, like the rest of their team. He remained a silent partner, which suited Jasper, never needing to deal with the awkward scenario of his brother-in-law bringing his sister to the club.

"You and your matchmaking. You're lucky you're damn good at it," Joanna said, bringing him back to the present.

"For others, sure." He winced at the slip. Under normal circumstances, Jasper could keep things locked down. This time, he opened the door for Joanna to pursue the subject.

"Listen, Jasper. Jess is-"

Jasper held up a hand, stopping his sister from saying anything else. "We're not discussing Jessica."

Joanna stared at him like she did as a teen despite their twelve-year age difference. Superior and all-knowing. "Three years have gone by."

Three and a half.

"Don't you want to be happy?"

"I am happy."

"You can't lie to me, Jasper. And I'm disappointed you'd even try."

"I'm not lying. I picked up the pieces, and I have a great life. Work, friends, you, Jonathan, and little Janie to spoil. It's all quite fulfilling. I promise I'm good."

He heard the hollowness in his voice, and while everything he said rang true, his heart remained frozen in time.

"If I'd known this is how it'd turn out for the two of you when I introduced you-"

"No, Jo, don't say it. Jess is it for me. Whether I got twenty minutes or a lifetime...and while I preferred the lifetime, I'll never regret meeting her."

"Okay, I'll drop it." Her tone indicated she wouldn't for long. Then Joanna's demeanor shifted, and she bit her bottom lip.

Her gaze traveled over everyone there to celebrate her daughter and caught her husband's eye. Jon gave her a smile filled with love and devotion, but when she turned back to Jasper, worry filled her expression.

"Things are escalating over there, and I'm helpless, tied up in bureaucratic limbo. After everything we've gone through to have our daughter, I'm afraid we're going to lose her, too." Joanna's voice cracked with emotion.

Jasper's courageous sister, who'd already suffered such tremendous loss, blinked back tears while he pulled her into a hug. He rubbed soothing circles on her back and held her tight. "I know. I'm ready to leave and get her when you have the paperwork. Hell. I'll get her out of there even if you don't."

Joanna and Jonathan suffered multiple losses until they decided on surrogacy to have a family. They went through a foreign agency, and their daughter was born amid the growing unrest in Ukraine.

"I check the status every day. All the authorities will say is they're working on it. The hospital she's in is safe at the moment, but...."

Yeah, he knew better than most. In rising conflicts, things can change in a heartbeat. Jasper clasped Joanna's hand in his. "You have my word, Jo. If things escalate, I will get Janie to you safe and sound, no matter what."

In the meantime, he'd pull whatever strings he possessed to speed up the process.

Joanna hugged him once more. "I know you will."

"Always, sister mine."

CHAPTER TWO

Jasper

As Jasper predicted, things escalated. The area where his niece was born turned into a full-blown Warzone. The hospital evacuated patients to a makeshift triage unit in the subway tunnels, doubling as bomb shelters beneath the city. It's past the time to get Sara-Jane home.

Jasper spent the past twenty-four hours calling in every favor he possessed to get the last forms needed to extract little Janie. Now, he functioned on caffeine and fumes, waiting for Grayson to arrive at the club. He rubbed a hand over his tired features when he heard a throat clear, followed by a knock on his open door.

"Hey, man. What's up?" Gray asked, stepping into his office. Jasper looked his friend over, his brother-in-arms, who he served with during countless missions and now ran Decadent alongside him. The man had never looked happier.

Whenever Jasper helped his family and friends find their special some-one, it filled a deep need within him, like some sort of purpose. "How are things with Addison?" he asked, eager to know. Gray's expression became one of love and adoration. It's a look Jasper remembered all too well.

"Addie and I...we fit. You know?"

His thumb moved of its own volition to the inside of his ring finger, tracing the letters of his one tattoo. *Jessica.* "Yeah, I know," Jasper said, pondering his 'gift,' never understanding why he knew certain people belonged together.

"...our temporary living arrangement is now permanent, with one condition," Gray said.

Jasper caught enough to ask, "What condition?"

Gray shifted his stance and crossed his arms over his chest. "Addie wants to buy the apartment we use in the city. It's a security thing for her, which I understand and am happy to concede. It also means I won't need your basement suite much longer."

The basement apartment is separate from the rest of his brownstone in Brooklyn Heights, and he enjoyed having Gray stay there a few nights a week. It made the place seem less...empty. "It's yours and Addison's. For the time you need it."

"Thanks, though I don't believe an update on my love life is why you wanted to meet with me today. What's going on, Jas?"

Jasper turned away, unable to take the concern he saw in his friend's gaze. He knew he looked like shit. He tipped his chin toward the door, and Gray took the hint and shut it. "I need a favor."

"It's yours, brother."

Gray's earnest answer made Jasper chuckle. "Aren't you supposed to hear my request first?"

"Doesn't matter. Whatever you need, it's yours."

Jasper knew Gray meant every word. Any of his former team would say the same thing if they stood in his place, and he's damn thankful for every one of them. This time, their unit's former sniper, Weston Sharpe, has his back. Jasper needed Gray here.

"I know you and Addison would prefer to spend your time at Stone Barn, but I'll need you here for the next two weeks. I'm taking care of something out of the country, and I don't want to worry about the club while I'm gone."

"You know I'll be here, and it'll give Addie and me time to do some apartment hunting." Gray hesitated, then asked, "Are you gonna tell me what this is about?"

Jasper did his best to clear the emotion clogging his throat and said, "Jo and Jon's surrogate gave birth to their little girl four weeks ago."

"They have a daughter? Why didn't you...?" Gray's question trailed off, and Jasper realized he thought the worst. Under the circumstances, Jasper understood why.

"Is their daughter okay?"

"So far, yes."

"What do you mean, so far?"

"The agency they worked with and their surrogate are in Ukraine."

"Oh. Oh, shit," Gray exclaimed when the full scale of what this meant hit him.

"Oh, shit is right, brother. The three of us are taking the red-eye into Heathrow, then I'll catch a flight to Poland."

"You can't do this alone. Let me go with you."

Jasper closed the distance between them and clasped Gray's forearm. "I need you here."

"You sure?"

"Yeah, I've reached out to West, and he's ready to help the moment I land." Jasper allowed Gray to pull him into a back-slapping hug he needed.

"Don't do anything stupid, like getting yourself killed."

"Don't worry, I have no plans to. Promise I'll be back in a week, ten days tops."

"Any longer, and I'll lead the cavalry to rescue your ass." With one more reassuring slap to his back, Gray let Jasper go.

Jasper smiled, knowing Gray meant every word. "I expect nothing less, brother." He gathered everything he needed from his office, shoved it into his messenger bag, and pocketed his wallet and keys. "Take care of our club, and I'll catch you on the flip side."

"You better."

Jasper tipped his chin in agreement, then checked the time on his phone. "Listen, I gotta go. I need to pack and catch a few hours of sleep."

"Watch your back," Gray called after him.

Jasper stopped in his doorway and said, "Always." He tapped the door frame and headed toward the back exit, eager to get this show on the road.

The couple of hours of shuteye Jasper caught at home will have to do. Any further sleep eluded him on the flight to London. The hushed, worried tones of his sister and Jon's conversation kept him alert, and he analyzed all the scenarios he might face on this precarious rescue mission until they landed.

Jonathan booked rooms at the Four Seasons, hoping its luxury spa or nearby Hyde Park would tempt Joanna to venture outside and not remain in their suite, staring at her phone for word of Sara-Jane's safety.

The worried look on his sister's face undid Jasper, and he hugged her. Joanna's grip on him was fierce while he told her, "You have my word, sister mine. I'll get Janie and protect her with my life until she's in your arms."

Jasper squeezed his sister tighter. "I need you to do something for me while I'm gone."

Joanna pulled back to look at him, tears brimming on her lashes. "What?"

"Don't stay locked up in this room riddled with anxiety while you wait for word from me. This is a big ask because I know how scared you are." Jasper stooped, meeting her gaze. "You can't worry yourself sick either. Be strong for your daughter, Jo."

"I know," Joanna said, tears spilling down her cheeks.

"I'll have my satellite phone, and all you need to do is keep your phone charged and with you," he said, encouraging her.

"The two of you deserve these moments with each other."

"Okay," Joanna said with a sniffle.

Jonathan tucked his wife to his side. "I'll make sure she does," he said, kissing Joanna's temple. Then Jonathan pulled him in for a one-arm hug. "Thank you, brother. For everything." His voice became gruff with emotion.

Jasper tightened his arms around his brother-in-law. "Take care of Joanna and keep her happy." He slung his pack onto his shoulder, eager to get to his niece. "Love you guys."

"Love you, too. Be safe."

"Always."

When the door to their room closed behind him, Jasper held his phone to his ear, and Weston Sharpe answered on the second ring. "West. It's time."

"I figured you'd call me any day. Things are going right to shite there. It's a damn shame. What do you need me to do, brother?"

The warm roughness of his voice with the hint of a Scottish brogue, thanks to the years living in Glasgow, put Jasper at ease. With West for backup, they'd have Sara-Jane in her parent's arms in no time.

"I'm headed to Heathrow. How fast can you get to RZE airport outside Gmina Medyka and pick me up?"

"Well...." Jasper heard West shuffling something in the background. "I'm in Prague. Seven hours, give or take."

"What the fuck are you doing in Prague?"

"Duh. Tattoo convention. I kept my ear to the ground, knowing you'd be calling me any day. I took a chance, and the convention dates worked out. Can you believe I'm an uncle now? Love that for me."

"Like fuck. I'm Janie's uncle," Jasper growled, despite knowing his friend ribbed him on purpose to take his mind off the severity of things.

"Dude, Joanna's like a little sister to all of us except for Jon, of course."

"For fuck's sake, West."

"Anyway, Jo sent me her latest pic, and their little angel will break hearts left and right. Don't you believe she's better off with all these extra uncles and a super kick-ass aunt around when suitors call?"

The instigator made a good point.

"Fine. You're Janie's uncle. Not her favorite, though, I am."

Jasper swore he heard West roll his eyes when he said, "Wouldn't dream of stealing your thunder."

"So, are we doing this or what?" Jasper asked, stepping into the lobby and catching the concierge's attention.

"Taxi, sir?"

"Please."

"Fuckin' right, we are," West replied, bringing Jasper back to their conversation.

"Meet you in a few hours then."

"I'll be there, locked and loaded. Catch you on the flip side."

CHAPTER THREE

Jasper

When Jasper landed and exited the terminal, he found West leaning against the fender of a Land Rover that'd seen better days. "How the fuck did you beat me here?" he asked when they embraced.

"I may have caught a ride on a private jet thanks to a certain A-list client I finished tattooing a sweet-ass piece on this week." He kicked the tire and slapped the hood of the rover. "Bessy here came stocked for all our needs, including this." West swung the back door open, revealing the car seat strapped inside.

"Fuck, West. I can't believe I forgot we'd even need...thank you," Jasper said with utter sincerity.

"When I say Bessy comes with everything. I mean ev-er-y-thing." West's laughter carried across the parking lot. "Ready to roll?"

"Damn right. The sooner we get there, the sooner we get Janie home. Joanna and Jon have gone through too much for them to lose their daughter now." Jasper tossed his pack in beside the car seat and closed the door.

"Aye, let's go. We've got an eight-hour drive ahead of us. Lots of time to chat and catch up." He got behind the steering wheel, letting Jasper know he'd have the next few hours to rest and prepare for his trek on foot to the tunnels leading to the bomb shelter beneath the city.

West hit him with the hard questions not five minutes into their drive. "Have you talked to Jess?"

What is with everyone these days?

"Fuck, not you, too. Between you and my sister, I can't get away from the inquisition. What about discussing our route or the plan when we get there?"

"Chill. Brother. Did you forget the part where I said there's an eight-hour drive ahead? We've plenty of time. By the way, there's no conspiring. Jess came to me two months ago for an appointment to finish her tattoo sleeve."

"Hold up. You've seen my wife? You've seen Jessica more than once and said nothing? What the fuck, West?"

"I've done her ink for the past couple of years. You mean you didn't know? Haven't you talked?"

"Jessica and I haven't spoken since the day she left."

"Wait. How did I not know this?"

"You're the one who's seen her. Why don't you tell me?"

"Fuck," West groaned. "The two of you have got to talk."

"Goddamnit, it's too late. Too much time has passed."

"You and I stay connected by text. I've seen Jess a handful of times when I inked her, and even I know the two of you still love the fuck out of one another. Haven't you both wasted enough time?"

Silence descended in the cab between them, and Jasper heard the pain in West's voice. "I'd give anything to have these years back with Maggie. Hell, I know she'd never want me wallowing. If you don't do it for your stubborn ass, do it for me and what I'll never get to have with her."

Jasper winced, and West took his eyes off the road, staring him down for an eternity until he refocused on driving. "Fuck, I'm sorry for my callousness."

"It's fine. I know you meant nothing by it. Not like you didn't have a shit time of it back then, too."

"Still isn't right." Jasper looked at his longtime friend, the pinched lines around his mouth visible in the dim light of the cab. Jasper also saw his strength and resilience. When they spoke in recent months, West sounded...good. Content even.

"She died more than a decade ago. I've made peace with it. Tattooing and therapy helped. I won't pretend it's easy because it's not. I've even dated here and there over the last few years. Nothing serious."

"Have you gone to any clubs? Played even?"

"I DM once a month, taking part in the community and indulging my voyeuristic needs. If you're asking if any lass or lad is calling me Daddy, the answer is no."

West and Kari need to meet.

Jasper didn't question the idea. Kari's a naughty brat with a heart of gold in need of a Daddy Dom, and West needs a 'lass' willing to bring excitement back into his life.

All Jasper needed to do was convince West to come home. "You know your membership remains active. You can even stay at my place. Better yet, Gray won't need the basement apartment much longer. Which means you'd have a place of your own to stay."

"Don't get carried away in making plans. We haven't finished talking about you, and have hours of driving ahead. You and I have plenty of time to discuss the good times we used to have."

West cleared his throat, his voice growing thick with emotion when he said, "And...and how Maggie would never want me to spend the rest of my life alone. She'd want me to be happy, Jasper...and I might be ready to be. So, I'll give your offer serious consideration."

"Wes-"

"I said, I'll think about it."

Jasper knew it hurt his friend to make such a monumental declaration. The future he'd planned forever altered the day Maggie died. Crazy how his and West's lives changed within a couple of months. His friend lost his wife weeks before Jasper's parents died, and he became Joanna's guardian.

"You've gotta talk to Jessica. Promise me, Jas," West pleaded after a few minutes of silence.

Damn it. West is right.

Even if it meant getting his heart ripped from his chest all over again. Good or bad, he needed to speak with Jessica. They both deserved closure or...fuck. He didn't want to contemplate the other possibility.

"Somewhere along the way, the two of you got your wires crossed, leading to some serious miscommunication," West muttered.

"What are you not telling me?" Jasper growled, the energy shifting between them.

Miscommunication?

Jasper's mind raced, and his heart rate kicked up.

"My tattoo chair is a sacred space, and it's not my story to tell."

Jasper wanted to rage about the injustice. "I can't believe it. I haven't heard a word from Jess since the day she left me with a written goodbye – a fucking note, West. Of all goddamn things," he roared, slamming his fist against the door panel and finding it reinforced. "Fuck," he bellowed some more, giving his hand a shake.

"Are you done now?" West asked. "Serves you right, anyway. Bessy didn't deserve your wrath. Please tell me you won't be retrieving Sara-Jane with a broken hand."

Jasper moved his fingers, finding them in working order. "What's broken is my ego."

If ego equaled his heart.

"Jasper, promise me you'll track Jess down and hash this out once we've gotten Sara-Jane to safety." West took one hand off the wheel and gripped his shoulder.

"You'll realize what's still there once you clear the air. Or what's not. At least you'll know."

The memories accosted Jasper. He came home, finding their brownstone eerily quiet, and called Jessica's name, searching each room until he found her note on the nightstand beside their bed.

His wife told him in a letter she wanted a clean break, and he respected her wishes by not contacting her. She'd used her safeword, knowing he'd never cross such a boundary.

Did he want to find her now? Yeah, he did.

"Let's get my niece, and then I'll consider searching for Jessica." Jasper sighed. "After all this time, I don't even know where to look."

West glanced over, offering him a cautious grin. "She told me she'd be in London the day after I finished her ink. I know it's not current info. At least it's a place to start."

When Jess left, she also left New York altogether, and now they might be in the same city after all this time? West's right. His intel is two months old, and who knows where she may be now, but Jasper wanted to find her.

"Alright. I'll stay a few extra days and check if Jessica's still around. It's the best I can offer." This conversation woke a desperate craving to glimpse her after all this time. To confirm she's okay.

"Good enough, brother."

Jasper closed his heavy lids and tipped his head back, wanting to focus on the mission, yet he drifted, and sleep pulled him under.

West hit a pothole and jarred Jasper awake. "Huh, what the fuck? You let me fall asleep?"

"Calm down. You seemed like you needed it. We're still ninety minutes out from your initial drop-off point. Figured you'd want to go over things and get ready."

Jasper stretched in his seat. "Any issues?"

"Nah. All clear. Folks seem to head in the other direction, and I don't blame them."

Jasper scanned their surroundings, taking in the deserted streets. "West, did I sleep through the border crossing?"

"Try not to get all growly when I tell you yes."

A rumble rose from deep in his chest despite his friend's plea. "Fuck, West."

"What? I gave them our papers, and they waved me through. At least now you're well rested and ready to rescue our sweet little niece."

"I needed to be alert while we made our way into rougher territory."

"Give me some credit, eh? We're all good. You're awake now. Let's go over the plan."

"Fine." Jasper opened his laptop to the file. "They moved the infants, each with a nurse, into the tunnels ten days ago. Five in total. Three were born to parents in the UK, and one to parents in Switzerland. Those children got extracted two days ago; Janie is the last one left."

"It can't be easy, being the last one to be evacuated. Is the nurse all right? They must be eager to make sure their loved ones are okay."

"Yeah, I guess. From what I gathered from Joanna, the ones who stayed with the babies volunteered."

"Huh, noble of them."

"Yeah, it was." Jasper tapped a few keys. "I've sent the GPS coordinates to both our watches, and you can track mine through this app," he said, pointing to the screen.

"You sure you don't want me to stash the rover and come with you?" West asked, stopping in an alley a few miles from the train tunnel Jasper planned to use. When he killed the engine, they both hopped out, and while Jasper rechecked his pack, West loaded and checked their weapons.

Mortar fire sounded in the distance, amping the need to get in and out fast. "I need you to stay with the vehicle. I'll call your SAT phone when I'm close to exiting the tunnels. You can move in and grab us quick."

Jasper gripped West's arm when he handed over his gun. "If anything happens...if we lose contact, or I take over five hours to let you know I've got her. You make sure she gets to Jo and Jon. Their daughter is priority one."

"Ten-four." West smacked Jasper's back. "Don't go doing something foolish like getting yourself killed."

"Never. Once I have Janie, I'll call you for a pickup. Easy-peasy."

"You fucking better."

"I will," Jasper reassured him. Then he cut across the alley and headed up the next street at a steady jog, keeping to the shadows.

Ukrainian soldiers patrolled the city in tanks, trucks, or on foot. He exchanged a few words with the guards at the entrance to the subway station.

With luck on his side, a guy he served with joined the Foreign Legion, fighting alongside them. The crazy bastard always ended up where they needed him. Daniels told him the fastest way to reach the area being used by the hospital.

Jasper came upon families huddled together, fear and wariness etched into their faces. He was glad he'd brought extra supplies, passing out bottles of water and snacks, giving them everything except what he needed for himself and his niece.

With each meager item he handed out, Jasper wished he'd brought more and vowed to send a large donation to Doctors Without Borders when he returned home.

The men shook his hand, and the women offered blessings and well wishes. "*Bud' zdorovyy. Dyakuyu tobi*-Bless you. Thank you."

The children stared at him with wide, innocent eyes despite the terror thrust upon them. This is not the first time he's seen the horrors of war. Each time he witnessed others' inhumanity, the boy inside him wished for superhero powers to save everyone he encountered.

He can't, though. His sole focus needed to be getting his niece out of there.

Jasper came to an area bustling with injured people filling curtained hospital beds, offering little privacy while the harried hospital staff rushed about.

A man with a clipboard approached Jasper with caution. "*Vy potrebuyete likuvannya*-Do you need medical treatment?"

Jasper understood the 'do you and medical' to get the gist of the man's question. "*Ni. Ya shukayu-uh-dytynu*-No, I'm looking for a baby. Uh...born to a surrogate-*Surohat*?" The man's brow furrowed, deciphering his choppy Ukrainian.

After a moment's contemplation, he nodded. "Tak, *Amerykans'kyy*-Yes. American?"

"*Tak*-Yes."

The man pointed toward an archway tucked away from the chaos of the makeshift hospital. "*Za rogom tam*—Around the corner, there. *Uspikhiv u spilkuvanni z upertoyu amerykankoyu*-Good luck dealing with the stubborn American woman."

Jasper caught the words 'luck, stubborn, and American woman' but did not get the chance to ask the man to clarify. He scurried off when another doctor called for him. "Uh, *Dyakuyu tobi*-Thank you," Jasper called after him.

He walked toward the archway and rounded the corner, finding the lighting dimmer and no one about. He moved further into the tunnel. Coming to the next bend, he heard someone humming. "*Pryvit*-Hello?"

"*Tykho bud'laska, ty rozbudysh dytynu*-Quiet please, you'll wake the baby." Came the annoyed whisper from within. He swore he heard her grumble, "Babies need their sleep, and this place isn't helpful. Shh, sweet girl, I got you." Something about the familiar, gentle tone drew him closer.

"*Vibach*-Sorry." Jasper lightened his steps. "You speak English? My Ukrainian has limits." The man with the clipboard said something about an American woman....

"Yes, I speak English." The woman answered when he rounded the corner, and for a moment, everything out of balance in Jasper's world clicked into place.

"Jasper?" The way she gasped his name created a familiar ache, and every bit of oxygen disappeared from the room with the sound. Then his lungs filled, and his world shifted off-kilter once again.

"Jessica Jones," he growled. And no, he didn't mean Marvel's reluctant superhero, despite her striking resemblance to the actress who portrayed her. "You never call. You never write...well, I suppose you wrote me once."

Jess dared to give him a defiant tilt of her chin and struck back with a jab of her own. "It's Jessica Harris."

"Our marriage certificate says otherwise, my darling, wayward *wife*. What the fuck are you doing in the middle of a war zone?"

CHAPTER FOUR

Jess

No, this isn't possible. No, no, no, no. Jasper's not real. How did her husband find her? Is this a dream?

Jess peered at the sleeping baby cradled in her arms, and the bottom dropped out of her stomach.

Is the baby his? Has Jasper moved on? Why hasn't he filed for divorce?

Why hasn't she?

Jess needed to use her voice and ask the vital questions aloud. "Is she yours?" she blurted.

Great. Start with the easy ones, Jess.

"Answer my question first." Jasper's gaze trailed from hers to her lips, to the baby, and back again, making her skin heat while the little angel in her arms slept on, unaware of the rising tension in the room.

"Let me put her down." Jess turned and bent over the crib and took a deep, steadying breath, which did nothing to quell her nerves. She'd need a lot more time to gather her strength to keep her walls up against this man.

Jess avoided facing Jasper a little longer, setting the baby in the bassinet and tucking her in. "I signed up with MSF or Doctors Without Borders not long after...um, anyway, this is my third posting."

Did he hear the hitch in her voice?

Of course, he did. Jasper missed nothing, which meant Jess couldn't hide anything from him. It's why she ran. Packed two bags, wrote Jasper the most agonizing words, and left everything else behind, unable to face his disappointment or the inevitable shift to resentment.

What if it didn't?

Jessica walked away without giving Jasper a chance. Now, she didn't believe she deserved one for herself. Every second in his presence highlighted the horrible mistake she'd made when she walked away.

"They stationed a group of us in Poland, and we moved in with supplies two weeks after the conflict escalated. They tasked us with setting up down here, and when things got worse, we moved patients into the tunnels."

"With my pediatrics training, I helped with the children and newborns, staying to look after the infants born via surrogacy, waiting for their parents."

"Jess."

"I didn't do this alone. Once the other babies got rescued, the other volunteers left with them, and I stayed behind to care for this little one."

"Jessica."

She took a shuddering breath. The heat coming from Jasper's body alerted her when he closed the distance between them. The way he growled her name...God, he's drowning her in his pheromones. She needed him like air, yet she put some much-needed distance between them.

No one else makes her this wild. No one else can fulfill her needs like he can. And Jess needed to come.

"Jessica, turn around." Jasper stilled behind her, waiting for her to move, and then she heard his whispered plea. "Please, Jess."

Jessica's breath caught, and her nipples hardened, the sensitive tips rubbing against the lace of her bra. Jasper's proximity alone brought her to the edge. He didn't need to touch her.

No., they can't go there.

Jess cleared her throat and crossed her arms, trying to hide what Jasper did to her. She turned and found him peering at the sleeping angel in the bassinet with a look of pure love.

It's a look she remembered well.

"I keep calling her angel. What's her name?"

When Jasper turned his captivating hazel eyes on her, his expression remained guarded, softening when he looked back at the sleeping baby. "Her name is Sara-Jane."

Jessica's heart ripped open when Jasper reached around her, brushed the tip of his finger across Sara-Jane's forehead, and said, "I can't get over how perfect she is. My sweet Janie."

"Ah, you stuck with the J names, after all." Married to him and having a J name herself, Jess knew of their family's running joke and odd tradition.

Jasper chuckled, a low rumble coming from deep in his chest. Jess loved how he laughed, never believing she'd hear it again.

Oblivious to her musings, he answered her initial question. "Not quite. Since I'm her favorite uncle, Joanna is...letting me call her Janie."

"This isn't your child?"

"No, Jess. She's not your child; therefore, she's not mine."

Don't cry. Don't cry. Don't cry.

"She's Joanna and Jonathan's daughter?"

"Yes."

"But why?"

"There's a lot you've missed since you left, and if you want to know, you need to ask Joanna yourself." The way his voice grew colder with each word he spoke sent a shiver down her spine.

"I...it's what I deserve."

Jess swallowed hard when Jasper lifted his hand toward her, and she braced for his touch. Then he pulled back and shoved his fingers through his hair at the last moment.

"Look, I'm here to get Sara-Jane for them. She's not mine, Jess. A child with anyone else is not something I want."

And there's the heartbreaking reason Jessica left Jasper three and a half years ago. She can't get pregnant.

"Listen-" Sara-Jane woke with a cry. Whatever else Jasper might've said got lost in the rumble of an airstrike hitting close enough, the ground shook beneath their feet. "Shit. How quickly can you have her ready to go?"

"Ten minutes, tops," Jess replied, grabbing some diapers, wipes, pre-made bottles of formula, and a couple of extra blankets. She tried to fit it in with her stuff when Jasper shrugged his pack off and handed it to her.

"Put what you need in this."

"You brought a car seat?" He'd strapped it to the outside of his pack.

"Yup." Jasper gave her an odd look and didn't elaborate further. Did Joanna send him with it? Jess shrugged and double-checked what she packed to ensure she missed nothing.

"Do you have her hospital records? I need her documents to get across the border. Please tell me you have your passport and visas with you."

"The red file folder on the counter is everything they sent with her. And I always carry an emergency pack with my documents, first aid kit, a change of clothes, bottled water, and protein bars," Jess said, patting her much smaller knapsack. "I don't go anywhere without it."

"Smart girl."

Jess blushed and bit her bottom lip. Still a sucker for his praise. Jasper handed her the folder, which she slipped into the pack behind the supplies.

Jasper scooped Sara-Jane into his arms, and everything inside Jessica melted. He made her seem even tinier, laying her against his chest to rub her back in soothing circles. "It's alright, sweet girl. Uncle Jasper's got you, and I won't let anything happen to you or Auntie Jess."

The look he gave Jess brokered no arguments.

Sara-Jane's cries calmed into little whimpers, and Jess wanted to whimper, too. *Auntie Jess*? She didn't deserve such a title.

She'd never get the image of this giant, imposing, powerful man, the one she'd love forever, holding this tiny, beautiful baby with a look of complete love and adoration on his face. Because Jess knew with heartbreaking certainty, she'd never give him the children he wanted.

Jasper kissed the top of Sara-Jane's head and lifted his eyes to Jessica's. He held her gaze, knowing his effect on her.

Damn it.

Jess fumed, while Jasper strapped Sara-Jane into the carrier with surprising ease.

"You ready to head out?" Jasper asked like he didn't turn her heart into a puddle of goo. "There's a vehicle waiting to pick us up when we get out of these tunnels."

Jess looked around the makeshift hospital room. If she left, there'd be one less person to help those who remained here. "I should stay."

"Like fuck you are," Jasper whisper-shouted. Then another missile struck, this time closer, sending a more intense tremor beneath them. "I'm getting the both of you out of here. There's no arguing about this, Jess. You won't win." He shrugged off his flak jacket and handed it to her. "Put this on."

Jessica knew this didn't follow protocol, so she scrawled a quick note explaining how she evacuated with the patient and said she would check in once they got to safety.

This is the closest she's come to experiencing what Jasper did during his military service, and she reached her limit. Jess needed to sleep for a week, get a proper meal, and then figure out what to do next.

Jess strapped the too-big vest onto her body, catching a hint of his woodsy scent. She bit her lip, fighting the urge to moan. When Jess controlled her emotions better , she cleared her throat and told him, "I'm ready."

Jasper took out his satellite phone, and when the person on the other end picked up, he said, "I got them. Meet us at the tunnel entrance. We'll be there in twenty minutes tops."

Jess swore she heard the man on the other end of the line ask, 'Them?' when he hung up. Jasper grabbed his bag and the baby carrier. "Let's go."

They headed out, keeping a quick pace, and Jess stayed on Jasper's heels. When they neared the entrance, Jasper raised his hand, stopping them. He turned and passed her, Sara-Jane. "I need you to carry her."

"Of course," she said, taking hold of the handle. Jasper pulled his gun from its holster, and she tried not to let fear overtake her.

"Stay behind me and do what I say."

"Okay."

"Say it, Jess."

Her heart rate kicked up, and she tightened her grip on the carrier. "I'll do what you say."

"Good girl."

Fuuuck!

They moved at a quick pace until they reached the street. With darkness surrounding them, the sounds of war grew louder, and Jess gripped the back of Jasper's shirt with her free hand.

She heard him say over the roaring of her heartbeat, "Don't worry, Jess. I got you."

A set of headlights flashed at them from the alley to their left. "This way." Jasper hurried them across the street and opened the back passenger door.

He grabbed the carrier from her outstretched hand and secured it behind the driver's seat. "Get in."

"We're rescuing more than our niece?" An all too familiar voice said from inside the cab. With Jasper here, Jess should've known.

"Hey, West," she said when she climbed in, and Jasper shut the door behind her before climbing into the front seat.

West gaped at her. "Jess?"

About to laugh at the irony, West beat Jessica to it. He looked between her and Jasper in the dimming interior light and howled with laughter. Not missing a beat, he threw the rover into gear and took off down the back streets away from the imminent threat.

But alone in a vehicle with the man she loved more than anything and the man who knew the real reason she left him is a whole different kind of danger.

"For fuck's sake, West," Jasper grumbled.

"It's...I mean-" West choked out between gasps. "Did we Beetlejuice Jess into existence?"

"Nope. Decided to surprise you both with a reunion. Though yours isn't as long in coming as ours."

Jess understood why Jasper's pissed. She also didn't miss the movie reference or what West meant by it. "You talked about me?" she asked, fear causing the tremor in her voice.

A disgruntled Jasper didn't quiet West's laughter. Jess's apparent fear, however, did.

"No, Jess. I'd never do that to you. It surprised me to learn you and Jasper haven't spoken in over three years," he said, staring her down through the rearview mirror.

"It's what happens when you walk away," she whisper-yelled, to not to wake Sara-Jane.

"Look, I told Jasper you need to talk, and I told him to look for you in London, nothing else. I swear."

"It seems I'm the one in this vehicle missing an important piece of the puzzle. Do either of you care to fill me in?" Jasper pivoted in his seat and glared at her, his eyes glinting under each streetlight they passed. His icy gaze instilled fear in anyone caught in it. Jess? It turned her on.

She ached for her husband.

Jess willed herself not to weaken and said, "No. There's nothing to say." Jasper's eyes filled with hurt, gutting her all the same.

"Uh, guys, you know I'm rooting for this reunion. But do you think we can put a pin in this discussion until you're alone and we aren't being followed?"

Jasper used his side mirror to track the vehicle twenty feet behind them. "Shit. Get down in your seat, Jess, and keep Janie calm. West is about to do some fancy-ass driving and get us the fuck out of here."

"Oh, ye of little faith. I'm already on it," West said, picking up speed while Jess slid to the floor, monitoring the tiny, oblivious angel who slept through it all.

Jess wished she'd fall asleep, too, and when she woke, they'd be out of harm's way.

Chapter Five

Jasper

A vehicle followed them until they reached the city limits. He and West figured them to be friends and not foes, though they didn't bother to stop and ask. They remained vigilant and kept conversation to a minimum.

When Jasper turned to check on Jess, she'd fallen asleep with her head against the window.

Lucky for him, West kept his mouth shut when he dug an extra shirt from his bag and tucked it under Jess's head. Her eyelids fluttered open, and for a split second, the world stood still. His breath caught when she smiled and snuggled into his shirt.

It left him bereft, trying to figure out how he'd survive when she walked away again. Jasper watched over her and Janie for the rest of the drive.

Jasper called Joanna when they reached the airport. She answered on the first ring. "Jasper?" Her voice trembled with emotion.

"Hey, it's me. Janie's safe, and in a few hours, you'll be holding her," Jasper said, rushing the words to let Joanna know she was okay. The sound of his sister's sobs broke his heart. "Sister mine...."

Joanna cried harder, and Jasper heard a commotion from her end and Jon's voice in the background.

"It's okay, sweetheart, I've got you." Then he came on the line. "Hey Jas, I'm going to put you on speaker. How's our baby girl?"

"She's amazing. Even sleeping through most of the excitement. It won't be long before we board our plane."

"You got a flight out right away?"

"West has the use of a private jet."

"Damn, he's resourceful."

"Yes, he is. We're out of here when they clear us for takeoff."

"Joanna and I will meet you at the airport."

"No. You stay at the hotel, and I'll bring Sara-Jane to you. Have a car service waiting for us, then you can be in a quiet space to bond with your daughter without dealing with the chaos of Heathrow."

"Yeah, good idea," Jon mumbled in agreement, though Jasper knew he wanted to do anything other than sit around and wait.

"Thank goodness we went out and bought some essentials today." Jon took a shuddering breath, and Jasper heard his sister's muted whimper. "We've waited a long time for this."

"I know." Jasper ached for them both. This wasn't the first time Jo and Jon had prepared for a child who didn't come home. "You won't go home without her. I'll protect her with my life until she's safe in your arms."

"I know you will. Thank you."

Jasper's gaze tracked around the airport hangar. West disappeared a while ago for caffeine and snacks, and Jess went to freshen up while he called.

Jasper's gaze froze on Jess when she exited the washroom on the other side of the deserted lounge. He let his gaze travel over her, memorizing every detail to hold dear when she disappeared on him again.

Jessica's eyes connected with his from across the room. She gave him a hesitant smile and closed the distance between them.

"Hey guys, I'm going to have to go. We'll be boarding any minute. Hang in there a few more hours."

"We'll try. Thank you for everything. Please be safe."

"Always. Oh, and Jo?"

"Yeah?"

Jasper was relieved to hear she'd stopped crying. "You're never going to guess who I ran into. Love you both."

"What? Who?" Despite all the drama that will come with Joanna finding out it's Jessica, Jasper chuckled and hung up the phone, knowing it was something for his sister to fixate on during the next few hours.

They reached altitude, and the seatbelt indicator turned off when little Janie fussed up a storm. One whiff - one horrifying whiff, and Jasper knew what happened. A real-life version of the 'Guess what's in the diaper' game.

Oh, god.

Jasper gagged, covering his nose and mouth with his hand.

It didn't help.

How did such a tiny, perfect human emit something so...putrid?

Jess rolled her eyes, and Jasper itched to take her over his knee. Her eyes widened, and she took a step back. "Uh, I'm going to take care of the little stinker. She's hungry, too. Aren't you?" To which Sara-Jane cried a little louder. "Yup."

Jess looked at West and rolled her eyes again.

Damn it.

This time, she did it with a smirk on her lips, knowing what it did to him.

West had covered the lower half of his face with his sweater, doing his damndest to avoid the smell filling the cabin. "Is there a kitchen in this sky hotel?" Jess asked him.

"The galley's through the door. Bedroom and bathroom are back there, too." Came his muffled response, refusing to uncover his mouth.

Jasper didn't blame him.

"I'll change her and get a bottle ready."

"Can I feed her?" Jasper's earnest question caught Jess off guard. "I mean, I can change her, too. I always planned on being the dad who'd do those things without question. Now I'm the uncle who does those things, too."

Jess held his gaze, her dark eyes shimmering with unshed tears, and Jasper swallowed over the lump of emotion in his throat. They might've been parents themselves by now.

Jessica looked away first, breaking the spell. She cleared her throat. "Don't worry about it. One clean baby and a warm bottle coming right up." Then, she turned with Sara-Jane in her arms and headed to the back of the plane.

Jasper took a step to follow, and West grabbed his arm, shaking his head. "Let her go, man." He pulled his sweater from his face and sniffed the air, taking a deep breath when he realized the smell had disappeared.

"Listen, you need to give her time to get over the shock of coming face to face with you. How about you leave the serious conversation until after you've gotten little S.J. to her parents?"

Jasper sighed and ran his hand over his face, dropping into the soft leather chair beside his friend.

"When Jess finishes disposing of the nuclear device of a diaper, how bout I make us adults something to eat? Then we can try to get a couple of hours of shuteye. Fuck knows we all need it."

"Yeah, you're right." His chair faced the back of the plane, and he fixated on the door leading to the galley. "*Jess is back there*," the voice in his head screamed.

Jasper gripped the armrests harder. While he needed to give her space, he also wanted answers. Did she grow to despise their dynamic the way she said in her letter? Or is it something else?

Tears flowed the second Joanna opened the hotel room door to find Jasper holding Sara-Jane. Overjoyed and overwhelmed by her daughter's arrival, Joanna didn't seem to register Jessica or West stepping into the room behind him.

"Oh, my god. Our baby." She sobbed, taking her daughter into her arms for the first time. "Look how perfect she is, Jon."

Sara-Jane blinked at them with some sort of cosmic intuition, giving her parents a toothless smile of recognition, which some may equate to gas. They knew otherwise.

"She looks like you, love," Jon said, staring at his precious daughter in his wife's arms with a look of utter devotion.

Jasper's vision blurred, and he turned away, finding West and Jess overcome with the same emotions.

West shoved his hands into his pockets and cleared his throat, drawing Joanna's attention to him and Jess.

"Jessica?"

"Yup, it's me," she said with an awkward wave. "Hey, Jo, Jon. Congratulations. Sara-Jane is beautiful and an absolute dream to care for. You're both blessed."

"Thank you, but...." Joanna's gaze flipped between him and Jess. "Is this what you meant when you hung up on me, Jasper? Why didn't I guess this?"

"While your brother tried to distract you, it worked for less than five minutes, hon." Jon chuckled, wrapping an arm around Joanna, eager to keep them close.

Jasper didn't blame him.

But when Jasper opened his mouth to respond, Jessica beat him. "Yeah, it's crazy how the world works sometimes," she said, refusing to meet his gaze.

The world? More like fate, sweetheart. Jasper's intense glare spoke the words he didn't.

Joanna handed Sara-Jane to her eager father and wrapped Jessica in a hug. "I don't know how to thank you. You're the one who kept her safe, fed, and clothed? Jess, you loved and cared for her without knowing how connected you are to her. You're her guardian angel."

"They sent my team to Ukraine. Right place, right time. I guess." Jessica shrugged, doing her best to brush off the praise.

Joanna squeezed her tighter. "It's much more, Jess. You know it is."

When they hugged, Jess enveloped Joanna's tiny frame with her willowy height. Her head rested on Joanna's, and a bitter sensation washed over Jasper. Not wanting to dwell on how, when Jess walked away, she left her friendship with his sister behind, too.

Her actions hurt Joanna, yet his sister's embrace and words conveyed love and forgiveness.

"I'm glad I got to care for her. Sara-Jane's the angel, Joanna." Jess pulled back from their hug, and he saw her shutting down, preparing to make another escape.

No.

Not after all this time. He and Jess owed each other closure at least, though now that he'd laid eyes on her again, he hoped like hell they'd do the opposite.

West swooped in for a couple of hugs. "Congrats, guys. Glad I can help deliver my little niece into her parent's arms. Maybe I have a chance at being crowned favorite uncle after all," West said with a wink, doing his best to dispel the growing tension.

"Not a chance, asshole," Jasper growled, not taking his eyes off his wayward wife.

"Jasper...language," Joanna scolded, and a second later, she said, "Oh, who am I kidding?" She kissed West on the cheek. "Thank you for having my brother's back and ensuring everyone made it out safe."

"Anytime. Say the word, and I'm there, lass."

It was at that moment Jessica made her escape attempt, slipping from their circle and taking a few steps toward the door.

"I'm exhausted and need to crash. It's great to...um, catch up with all of you. I'm glad your daughter is safe and with you where she belongs."

Jasper tracked her movements toward the door.

"Jessica, please wait," Joanna called after her, to no avail. His sister didn't have to turn her pleading gaze on him to kick him into gear.

"I'll come back later and say good night," he said. "Things with Jess can't wait. Not anymore."

Joanna touched his arm. "I know this is difficult, but please don't approach Jess with anger." She cautioned. "Even after all this time, you two can work this out."

Jasper looked at his sister. "I'll try." Then he gently shut the door so as not to startle Sara-Jane and took off after his wife.

Jasper's long strides swallowed the distance between him and Jess. Not a word from her in over three years, and he'll be damned if he lets his wife walk away again without the two of them talking, fighting, or fucking.

Preferably, they'd do all three.

CHAPTER SIX

Jess

Jessica needed to escape from this hotel room. Everything's closing in on her. The lack of sleep. Stress. Uncertainty. A literal goddamn war. And Jasper...coming face to face with him, being in his presence is too much.

Jess didn't know how to keep it together any longer. She needed a moment to herself. Needed to breathe and try to process all of it.

She's a coward.

Why? Why now?

"Fate," her inner voice whispered.

Jessica's hands shook, and she shoved them into the front pocket of her hoodie, trying to hide the tremors. "Don't run, don't run. Don't look like you're fleeing," she chanted to herself.

Of course, it created the opposite effect, and Jess picked up her pace.

She got about a dozen steps down the hall when she found herself sur-rounded by Jasper's heat and caged against a hotel room door. When he slid the keycard over the lock, the telltale beep let Jess know whose room she was being corralled into.

Coincidental and convenient.

For some ridiculous reason, the scene in Forrest Gump where he stops running and tells everyone he'd like to go home now popped into her head. Shit. Whether or not she's ready, Jessica's finished running.

But is she prepared to go home?

Jasper shut the door and flipped the lock the second they got inside. He leaned against it, blocking Jess from going anywhere until they got this out.

Each prolonged second of silence elevated the tension between them while he raked his gaze over her. It's like he touched her, and Jess feared her legs might give out.

"You're even more beautiful than the day we met."

God, his voice...his words.... Jess bit back a whimper. The rich rumble washed over her and set her skin ablaze. Her underwear dampened with her arousal, and her long-denied pent-up desire roared to life. The man is going to make her come by breathing the same air.

An orgasm over three years in the making.

It's like her body ceased to orgasm when she walked out their front door, and Jess took it like punishment for taking the coward's way out. It didn't mean she didn't try to the point of epic frustration. But no matter what 'guaranteed to get her off' device she tried; Jess never did.

How did she fight this? Why did she even want to?

It's fucked up, and Jess will need hours of therapy to unpack all of this.

Coiled tight and ready to combust if Jasper laid a finger on her. Jess needed space to think, to figure out how to tell him the truth. In fact, if she didn't get out of there, they'd have sex in an epic anger-fueled fuck-fest. No way will it be a good thing for either of them.

Jess carefully chose her words, attempting to talk her way out of this potentially disastrous situation. "Jasper, I know we need to talk. We're both exhausted, and I want to sleep for the next twenty-four hours. Isn't it better to have this discussion when we have clearer heads?"

In the blink of an eye , Jasper went from leaning against the door to standing in front of her. Mere inches now separated them. Jasper pressed his index finger to the base of her throat, where the V of her sweater bared her skin.

"There's a comfortable bed right over there," he said, tilting his head toward the king-size four-poster against the wall.

Damn. It did look comfortable.

Not the point, Jess.

His hazel eyes darkened, and he dipped his head a little closer. "We can both get the sleep we need right after I spread you out and give you the fucking we both crave."

Jess gasped, and her underwear flooded with arousal. She looked down when she didn't feel the warmth of his fingertip. Jasper held a folded piece of paper against her. It looked worn like he'd folded it a million times.

She knew what it was, recognizing the faded stationery. The sight of it broke her heart all over again.

"There's something I need first." The tip of his nose ghosted along hers as he spoke.

Jessica's panic escalated. With the letter between them, there's just one thing Jasper will want to know.

"I'll give you everything when you tell me why you left."

Giving Jasper the answer he deserves will shred her to pieces. Jess held his gaze, searching for the words she never wanted to say aloud while the paper pressed against her breastbone seared her skin.

Jess wanted to tell him. To unburden them both of the truth. The words remained lodged in her throat.

"Please don't make me. Not yet. I don't know how. Let me face the consequences of my actions later. Right now, I need you, Jas. Please."

If anyone can break her mental block, it's the only man who'd ever gotten her off. Jess let her gaze travel down his body and licked her lips with anticipation.

Jasper was hard.

"You want me, too." She missed the way his cock filled her in such a way it made her ache with need when he didn't. Desperation emboldened her words. "Fuck me and make it hurt."

Then Jessica did something that shocked them both. She gripped the collar of his green t-shirt and tore it open from neck to waist. All the while, his finger held the damn paper against her skin. Then he slipped the same hand around her throat.

Jess sucked in a breath when Jasper tightened his grip, trapping her letter of lies against her larynx. "Nice to know there are still some things you'll be honest about."

CHAPTER SEVEN

Jasper

Jasper squeezed her throat, avoiding putting any pressure on Jessica's windpipe, and then he examined the remains of his torn shirt. He unleashed a growl, encompassing everything he'd kept in check all these years, and crashed his mouth against hers in a punishing kiss filled with three and a half years of suppressed need.

With everything left unsaid, this won't end well for either of them. Their pent-up emotions crackled like electricity in the air. "You want this rough?" Jasper growled against her lips.

"Yes...please, sir-" Jasper tightened his grip, cutting her off. Jess gave up the moniker the day she walked out on him, and he needed to know why.

"You don't get to address me as sir. Not tonight. Not after all this time. If you want that to change like I fucking do, you'll tell me the truth, Jess. Either talk or unbutton my jeans and take my cock out."

Jasper held back his bitter laugh when Jessica reached for the button of his pants. He stopped her, deciding he'd take everything if this was his one chance. "Stop. Remove your clothes first. Show me what you've denied me."

Jasper released her throat, taking the note with him. He stepped back, allowing Jess to undress while he tucked the paper into his wallet.

"Yes, S-" Jess cleared her throat, catching herself when he stared her down. "Yes, Jasper."

"Better." He sat on the end of the bed to watch his wife strip off her clothes. She didn't waste any time kicking off her boots. She undid her pants, sliding them off along with her socks. "Pause," he commanded.

Jess stilled, dropping her hands to her sides, wearing her boyshorts and black hoodie.

Jasper stood and circled her, taking in what she'd revealed thus far. "Spread your legs and up onto your toes."

Jess shuffled her feet wider, raising up onto her toes like he demanded. Jasper pulled her underwear tight between her cheeks and rubbed the fabric against her pussy lips.

He leaned in and growled next to her ear, "I can hear how wet you are and taste your arousal in the air." Jasper took out his utility knife and flicked the blade open, pressing the flat side to her lower back. "Don't move."

Jasper dragged the knife across her skin, slicing her underwear at her hips. Jessica whimpered when he pulled them from between her thighs and pressed the wet material to his nose, breathing her in.

His tongue darted out, tasting her for the first time in years. "Fuuuck. The scent of your pussy is like coming home to me."

"Please, Jasper, I need you inside me."

"Take off the rest. Show me this pretty ink I've heard all about." While his needle phobia kept him from getting more, he loved tattoos on others. He imagined Jessica's designs to be works of art and wanted to memorize every shaded line.

Out of habit, he rubbed his thumb where her name's etched into his skin. Like his lone piece of ink, Jessica is it for him.

Jasper's gaze remained riveted to her while Jess clutched the bottom of her hoodie and pulled it over her head, dropping it to the floor beside her. Her black bra was the last piece of clothing she wore. "You're stunning."

Jess sported a half-sleeve tattoo on her right arm. Beautiful flowers, leaves, and vines in vibrant colors decorate her skin. A full sleeve covered her left in shades of black and grey, flowing from her inked wedding band up the length of her arm across her collarbone.

"It's West's best work I've seen yet. You are living art, Jess." Jasper's gaze moved to her covered breasts.

Were they still...?

"The bra, Jessica. Now."

"Yes, Jasper." Her fingers shook, and she fumbled with the clasp until it landed on the floor, baring her perfect breasts, and under the lamp, her piercings, the ones engraved with his initials, shone in the light.

She'd wear a chain connecting them if they had plans to go to Decadent. But like many of her belongings, she left the chain behind. "You still wear them, even after breaking our contract?"

Heat stained Jessica's cheeks, yet she gave him a stubborn tilt of her chin and said, "I'd need to find someone with the right tool to unlock them or ask you...so the rings stayed."

"The key you needed is still in the nightstand drawer on your side of the bed. Were you in such a rush to leave you didn't even remember you always held the power? Why use your safeword and leave without removing them when you'd have such a reminder of who you belonged to?"

Jess lost a bit of her fire, and the pain in her eyes cut him to the core. "I don't know what you want me to say," she said, filling the silence.

"How about the fucking truth?"

She whimpered, and her voice cracked. "I'm not ready."

"Over three years have gone by. How much time do you need? You know best, right? Why do you hold back part of yourself from me when we promised to give each other everything?"

"I don't know. Please, Jasper, I need more time."

Despite the pain to follow, Jasper planned to indulge. "Alright, Jess. On your knees." She dropped to the floor. "Now, you can take my cock out."

Jess lowered his zipper and pulled the waistband of his boxers down enough to free him. When she wrapped her fingers around him, Jasper shuddered in her grasp.

This is not supposed to be gentle for either of them.

Jasper brushed Jessica's hand aside and replaced it with his own, circling the base of his cock with his fingers. "You may have begged me to fuck you, but you didn't specify which hole." He tapped the tip of his cock against her lips, smearing them with precum and demanding she let him in.

Her eyes locked with his, and when her lips parted, Jasper fed Jessica his cock inch by inch. "Swallow and suck," he commanded.

Jasper wrapped her ponytail around his hand, ensuring Jess kept her gaze on him. "Slap my thigh if you need me to stop." Then he rocked his hip back and fucked her face. Hard.

Jess hummed and hollowed her cheeks to suck him to the back of her throat. Three years and seven months without her perfect cocksucking skills, and he's ready to explode.

Not. Yet.

Jasper pulled free from her swollen lips. "Thank me." He held his cock out of the way while she nuzzled his balls through the material, and he cursed his decision not to give her anything more than his dick.

"Thank you for fucking my face, Jasper. Please fuck my pussy."

Fuuuck. Jasper bit his bottom lip, hoping the sharp pain would pull him back from the edge of release her words pushed him to.

"Enough," he growled. "Get on the bed on your hands and knees with your ass in the air." Jess scampered onto the mattress, eager to do his bidding.

"Lift your ass higher," he commanded. "Present your pussy and beg me with your body the way you used to."

Jess arched her back and spread her knees wider. She pressed her face into the blankets while she gyrated her hips and mewled for him.

"Come on, Jess. You can do better. Beg me. How long has it been since you've come?"

She froze, and their heavy breathing filled the sudden silence.

"I've got a confession to make," he said when she said nothing, trailing his forefinger along the back of her left thigh.

"What?" she gasped.

"The last night we shared is the last time I've come."

"No."

"It's true." Jasper notched the head of his cock at her opening, gripping her hips hard enough to leave bruises. For endless moments he didn't move, waiting Jess out while her pussy tried to suck him inside.

The best and worst kinds of torture.

"Jasper?"

"Yes?"

"I haven't either. No matter what I do, I can't."

"I bet if you unburden yourself, it'll free you from what's stopping you from getting off."

"I-I don't know. Why haven't you?"

"Why? I waited for you. I meant what I said, Jess, you're it for me, and I'd wait a lifetime for you."

"Oh, God."

"I'm no god, Jess. I'm your husband, and you can tell me."

"Jasper, please…I can't. Please, fuck me."

"Stubborn till the end. Remember, this is what you asked for." Jasper thrust into her wet heat, giving into the need, though he knew it'd never be enough.

Jess gripped fistfuls of the comforter and buried her face in it, daring to hide from him. "Look at me," he commanded.

Jess flipped her dark hair out of her face and met his gaze. Jasper saw her inner turmoil reflected in her eyes.

"Why did you use your safeword?" He punctuated each word with a thrust of his hips, dragging his cock along her sensitive inner walls.

"I...." Jessica's words trailed off, and her lids drifted closed when he rocked into her and rotated his hips.

"Eyes on me." They snapped open, and she whimpered, giving him a glimpse of the pain she carried.

"At least answer me that."

"Because I...I knew you'd never cross such a boundary." Jess confessed with a body-shaking sob.

"You're right, and I didn't. This moment is a different beast. Your wanting me to punish you with my cock has decimated those lines. Now, why did you walk away from us?"

"No, Jasper. Please don't make me say it." Jess pushed her ass back against him, begging with her body for him to fuck her harder.

Everything has led to this moment. If Jasper wanted to ensure her pleasure and his, Jess needed to tell him the truth.

She may not be ready to admit what made her leave, but he planned to do his damnedest to fuck the truth out of her.

Thirty minutes or three hours may have passed, but neither seemed close to coming.

Jasper sensed Jessica's frustration; he felt the same, and they needed to stop. Otherwise, there'd be physical ramifications to go with the emotional torture they're already putting themselves through.

"Jess, we need to stop."

He pulled out of her pussy and rubbed his angry, unsatisfied cock against her ass, smearing their combined slick on her skin. Then, with an unsatisfied grunt, he tucked his aching dick back in his pants.

"Looks like neither of us is getting off tonight."

Jess pressed her face into the pillow and screamed in frustration.

"You and me both, sweetheart," he said when Jess ran out of steam and her voice gave out.

"All you gotta do is tell me the real reason you left, and I'll fill this beautiful cunt to the brim with my cum, and you'll get the orgasm of your life."

CHAPTER EIGHT

Jess

J ess lifted her face from the pillow she'd screamed her heart and soul into. Frustrated tears tracked down her cheeks when she met Jasper's gaze and snapped.

"Is this how you punish your subs and yourself? I never took you to be a masochist, Jasper."

"I have one submissive. One wife. There are no others." Jasper went to his duffel bag and pulled out a fresh shirt, tossing the one she'd ruined into the garbage.

"I'd like to counter with the note you left me after what turned out to be your goodbye fuck because I never took you for a sadist." Then he zipped up his bag and looked around the room.

"Are you leaving?"

"Yup. I'm going to talk to Jo and Jon. Check on Janie one more time, and then I'm going home. You remember our home, don't you? I'm still there despite it being like a tomb since you left. I'll be there or at the club. Find me when you're ready."

Jasper grabbed his stuff and said, "The room's paid for until the end of the week." Then she heard him mutter, "Fuck it." Jasper threw his bag on the floor and stepped into her space. He cupped her face and stared into her eyes, baring his soul to her.

"I love you, Jess. I've never stopped. You're it for me, and when you remember I'm it for you, we can get on with our happily ever after." Jasper dropped his hands and stepped back, the absence of his touch wrecking her more.

But it's what she deserved.

"Jasper, wait. Please," she begged, struggling to get her numb limbs into the clothes she discarded on the floor.

How did she say it? How did she tell him?

He stopped, not looking at her. "Unless the next words out of your mouth are the real reason you left...well, I won't tolerate any more lies. You know where to find me when you're ready." Jasper unlocked the door and flung it open.

Ever the protector, he said, "Lock the door behind me."

Jess grabbed the door with her heart in her throat, keeping it from closing. "Jasper, please, I don't want to hurt you, I-"

"It's too late, Jess. You already have."

"No, Jas, please...." Her eyes burned with fresh tears because Jasper had walked away from her this time.

Jasper took off down the hall when West came off the elevator. Her teeth sank into her bottom lip until she tasted blood while the two men exchanged words. No doubt, the conversation was about her.

West cast a worried glance her way after every other word Jasper spoke. They hugged, and then Jasper knocked on his sister's door.

She and West stared at one another until Jasper disappeared into his sister's hotel room. Jess covered her mouth. It didn't stop the sob from escaping.

She might've collapsed in the hall if West hadn't grabbed hold of her. He helped her back into the room and closed the door behind them.

"Hey, now. I got you. Shhh...it's okay." West rubbed soothing circles on her back, and Jess cried, allowing herself to sink into her friend's comfort.

"I know everything is taking a toll on you. Being caught in a war zone, keeping Sara-Jane healthy and safe, and then coming face to face with Jasper. The emotional turmoil you must be in, I can't imagine."

"I don't know how to wrap my head around it. Wh-what did he say to you?" Jess hiccupped and sniffled. "Ugh, I need a tissue."

"Hold on a sec. Don't snot all over the place," West said. Jess snorted, making a snot bubble.

"Oh my god, don't make me laugh. You're making it worse, and this is the least mortifying thing I've experienced in the past twenty-four hours."

Jess snatched the tissue West held out for her and blew her nose. He offered another, which she used to soak up her tears. "Thank you." She groaned and tipped her head back to stare at the ceiling. "Please tell me what he said, West."

The desk chair creaked with his weight, and West rubbed a hand over the scruff on his face. "He didn't say much, Jess. Told me I was right and the two of you needed to talk. He also figured you'd stick around here for a while and asked me to make sure you're okay. So, I'm asking. Are you okay?"

Jess flopped back onto the rumpled bed, which smelled of Jasper and her. "Fuck, no. It's too late for us, isn't it?"

West's blond hair fell across his forehead. He brushed it back when he leaned forward and clasped his hands between his thighs, pinning her with his pale blue gaze. "I don't believe it's ever too late with the two of you."

Jess didn't want to hope, yet Weston Sharpe made her hope.

"While Jasper slept most of the drive, we did have a chance to talk. The funny thing is, it worked both ways. I told him, it's time I tried to move on, and he told me, he hasn't heard a peep from you since the day you left."

"He didn't come after me either," Jess said, dropping her head back to the mattress, breaking West's penetrating gaze.

"Are you fucking kidding me right now, Jess? You used your safeword in a Dear-fucking-John letter, breaking your relationship. Fuck. Gray said Jasper was a fucking mess for weeks after you left. Burying himself in work, trying to ignore the literal hole in his chest because he didn't know how to live without you."

She covered her face with her hands, covering the fresh tears trickling into her hairline. "God, I fucked up. Like, in the worst possible way. I don't deserve his forgiveness."

West crossed the room and pulled her hands away from her face, tugging her into a sitting position. "You received a devastating diagnosis, and while Jasper got hurt, he'd never fault you for how you dealt with it. Does this mean you're ready to tell him the truth?"

Jess mulled his question over. The many shocks of the past twenty-four hours wore her down, and she realized her running days were over. "Yeah, I am. He deserves to know the truth."

"Why did you tell me when you couldn't tell him?"

Jessica's cheeks heated with a blush. "To test a theory."

"What theory, Jess?"

"Yeah...um, I wanted to find out if telling someone solved this issue I have, and I'd get over this mental block thing and be able to...uh, have an orgasm again." Jess finished whispering, fearing her face must be scarlet by now.

"What?" West's eyes widened when what she said registered. "Oh...oh, shit. It didn't work, did it?"

"Nope," she said, emphasizing the P. "It didn't."

West pulled Jess into another hug. "I'm not sure you have a mental block. I believe it's more of a Jasper block."

West leaned back and searched her gaze. "Tie up any loose ends you have here, and then get your ass home. Repair things with Jasper once and for all. Then I'll bet you'll be having all the orgasms your heart desires."

Jess laughed and hugged him tighter. "I'm glad Jasper has you for a friend. I'm glad you're mine, too."

"Promise me you won't waste any more time with things left unsaid between you two."

West knew better than anyone about life's regrets, and Jessica intended to keep this promise. "You have my word. I'll tell Jasper everything."

"Secrets have a way of coming out, Jess. Make sure he hears the truth from you."

CHAPTER NINE

Jasper

The car service dropped Jasper at his doorstep, and he trudged up the steps. Jet lag and the complete emotional upheaval of being near Jess...inside her, fucked with his head.

He didn't bother with the lights, tossing his bag on the floor inside the door. He let the dim glow through the gap in the curtains guide him to the liquor cabinet.

The plan?

To lose himself in the sweet oblivion of alcohol. To hell with a glass. Jasper popped the lid off a bottle of Black Label and took a long pull, letting the whisky burn a path straight to his gut.

"Fuck." He still smelled her. Still tasted her. The memory of her pussy clenching around him...neither of them finding satisfaction, and both admitting they've lived a chaste life for over three years.

Jasper may not know why Jess left; he knew she loved him the way he still loved her.

For the millionth time, guilt consumed him over leaving Jess behind in London, but...she used her safeword. She'd run from their marriage as if someone chased her.

What made Jessica believe there was no other solution? Why didn't she confide in him? Until she left, he understood them to be open and honest with one another, yet questions like these had run on a loop in his head since the day she disappeared, and it didn't get him any closer to an answer.

If there's a chance for them to be together, Jessica needs to be the one to instigate it. Perhaps fate gave them a shove, putting them together in Ukraine, but it's not enough. Jasper craved more.

The alcohol didn't have the desired effect, and memories accosted him from every direction. Jasper stumbled from the living room into the kitchen. He grabbed the counter to steady himself while he took another swig and stared out the window into their tiny yet perfect backyard.

They dated through Jess's last year of university, buying this house together the month after she graduated.

"Welcome home, baby."

"Is this real?" Jess exclaimed, jumping into his arms. She wrapped her legs around his waist and her arms around his neck, gazing at him from beneath her lashes. She perfected this look from the first time she'd looked up at him from on her knees.

Jasper growled, kissing her while he walked them inside, not stopping until they reached their bedroom on the third floor, and he laid her out on the mattress the movers had dropped in the middle of the room hours earlier. He stared into her eyes, and she stared right back. "I love you, Jess."

"I love you, too."

He leaned over the kitchen sink and stared into the darkness. Yet it's not the darkness he saw. They'd gotten married right out there. Jasper wanted to give Jessica the most elaborate wedding. She wanted a simple and intimate affair, and he conceded.

"Do you, Jessica, take Jasper to be your husband, to love and cherish from this day forward, for as long as you both shall live?"

Tears shimmered in her eyes, and he caught a wayward one with his thumb when he cupped her cheek.

"I do."

"And do you, Jasper, take Jessica to be your wife, to love and cherish from this day forward, for as long as you both shall live?"

A lifetime isn't long enough. "I do."

"Then, by the powers vested in me by the state of New York, I pronounce you husband and wife. You may now kiss one another."

"You don't have to tell me twice," he said while their loved ones cheered and hollered. Jasper touched his forehead to hers. "Well, wife? May I kiss you?" he whispered.

"Please, husband."

Jasper didn't wait a second longer to capture her lips in a searing kiss.

After the ceremony, West used Jasper's home office to set up his portable tattoo equipment and gave them their forever bands.

Jasper stumbled out of the kitchen toward the stairs, leaving his memories and the bottle of whiskey half-finished on the counter.

Jasper used the banister to steady himself until he reached the second floor. They'd spent little time here, their primary suite being on the third. They planned for their children's rooms to be on this floor. To this day, the three bedrooms remained empty and undecorated.

Cold reality hit him. The image of Jess rocking Sara-Jane in her arms popped into his mind.

Jasper stumbled against the wall, where he caught and steadied himself. Is the reason Jess left because they didn't have children? He slid down the wall until his ass hit the floor, and his head thudded against the drywall.

After all this time, is it such a straightforward yet utterly complex answer?

He loved to fuck Jess bare. Having the wet heat of her pussy surrounding his flesh drove him wild. And with Jess not on the pill or opposed to the possibility. Jasper figured if it happened, it happened, and they'd be happy about it when it did.

Except it never did.

Jasper sifted through his memories of the months leading up to Jess leaving. Joanna and Jon got married. How quiet she got when Jo talked about having kids.

This is some hindsight *twenty-twenty shit.*

It's not an excuse. In the first few years after the club opened, Jasper worked long hours to achieve its current success. Jess worked shifts at the hospital, and their precious time together deepened their dynamic yet....

Jasper sometimes caught her in tears, which she tried to hide. Or he'd find her staring off into the distance with a look of sadness on her face. When he asked Jess about it. She tried to hide it, giving him a smile and telling him she was tired from her shift.

He prided himself on his insight. And to admit, even to himself, he'd missed this, gutted him. Didn't Jess know he loved her, no matter what? Children, no children. If she's by his side, nothing else matters.

Maybe he's the one who can't give her what she desires.

Why didn't she file for divorce?

Fuck.

Thump, thump, thump....

A dull ache formed at the back of Jasper's head, the alcohol wearing off enough for him to realize he sat there, banging his head against the wall. Whatever happened in the past, he'd have no definitive answer until Jess confirmed his theory.

Jasper rubbed his eyes with the back of his hand, though it did nothing to stem the tears slipping down his cheeks. What if Jess didn't come back?

CHAPTER TEN

Jess

Jessica rang the doorbell and kept her breathing steady, trying not to let the panic consume her while she waited. It'd taken longer than she expected to get back.

Was she too late?

Her debrief with DWB held some awkward moments thanks to her abrupt departure, though it concluded on a positive note. Thanks to a sizable donation being made in her name.

Jasper.

All the ways he showed how he cared for her drove her mad and made her swoon.

When the cab dropped her off on her mother's doorstep last night, Jess received hugs and kisses, a home-cooked meal, and one hell of a mother-daughter heart-to-heart fueled by two bottles of wine.

Then, her mother gave her one more hug and some parting advice before sending her to bed.

"I've never witnessed someone love another person as fiercely as Jasper Jones loves you. If you believe there is someone out there better for him than you, you're a fool. And I know I didn't raise a fool."

It took Jess a long time to fall asleep.

Jess stood on the porch, bracing herself for the footsteps she heard approaching from the far side of the door.

Okay, here goes nothing. What if Jasper's here? Their place is four blocks away. What if he's not? Did she want him to be? Will it be easier if he is?

The door swung wide, stopping any further debate or self-doubt. "Hi."

She surprised Joanna, who held Sara-Jane in one arm while she held the door open with the other. "Jessica? What a surprise. I didn't know you're back. Come in, come in." Joanna ushered her in and closed the door behind them.

Jess spent a lot of time here over the years, having met Joanna in her second year of university when they roomed together. They became fast friends, and when she confided she'd be spending the holidays alone because her mom took care of her Grams after hip surgery, Joanna invited her to spend Christmas with her and her brother.

One look at Jasper, and Jess fell. Hook, line, and sinker.

"Come to the kitchen," Joanna said, jolting her from her memories and leading the way. "I'm about to feed this little one. Can I get you something to drink first?"

"No, I'm good, thanks. Sara-Jane has flourished in the weeks since I've seen her." Jess smiled and made silly faces at Sara-Jane. "Any issues? Is she eating and sleeping well?"

"Her sleep pattern is a little off, then again, so is mine. She seems to be settling into a routine, at least." Joanna settled Sara-Jane into her highchair.

"We took her to the pediatrician yesterday for her three-month checkup, and she's hitting all her milestones like a champ."

"She's resilient, like her mom."

Joanna reached over and squeezed her hand. "Thank you. Thank you for all you did to keep our daughter healthy and safe."

Jess never did well with being singled out like this, shifting the attention back to Joanna. "I'm ecstatic for you and Jon. I always knew you'd make amazing parents."

"It's the same thing I believed about you and Jasper."

"Is Jon here?" Jess asked, peering down the hall, trying to change the subject.

"Nope. Sara-Jane and I are having a girl's day. Jasper's not here either, in case you were wondering." Joanna cooed at her daughter. "Did Jasper tell you how we partnered with a Ukrainian surrogacy agency?"

For all the scenarios she ran in her head, this is not how Jess imagined their conversation would go. "No, he didn't. We haven't exactly done a lot of talking."

Joanna's gaze searched hers when she said, "No. I suppose you haven't. From what I hear, you haven't talked to anyone except West since you left."

Jess swallowed the pain from her sister-in-law's blunt delivery. She deserved it.

Joanna expelled a deep breath and gestured toward the kitchen island. "Grab a stool and get comfortable. I won't linger on the darkest details because it's a bit of a sad tale. However, it has a guaranteed HEA," she said, kissing Sara-Jane's downy auburn curls.

"I love a happy ending." Jess still hoped to find her own.

Joanna gave her a soft smile and fed Sara-Jane the last tiny spoonful of her mushy cereal. "Don't we all." She grabbed the bottle from the warmer on the counter, gave it a shake, and tested it on her wrist. Sara-Jane gave a contented little snuffle and settled against her mother to finish her lunch.

"You've been gone a long time."

Despite her heartbreak over not having children, the way she handled finding out she can't hurt many people she cared about.

"You're right. I have, and you've every right to be angry. I'm sorry for the pain I've caused you. Once I left, it became easier to stay gone as more time passed. Ugh...I hope I'm not fu-forking this up. You know I'm not great at expressing myself."

"No kidding." Joanna teased her with a pointed look. "And don't worry about curbing your language. She's too young to understand, and by the time she's old enough to talk with the number of alpha males in her life, I'm resigned to accepting the word fuck will be one of the first she says."

Joanna's expression turned somber. "You need to know you didn't destroy him, Jess. Jasper's waited for you. A lot has happened since then, and it's time you knew some of it. You're one of my dearest friends, and this will hurt to hear like it'll hurt to tell you."

Jess fought her tears. She deserved this pain, abandoning her friend when she needed her the most. Joanna's eyes appeared extra shiny, too, and she reached over and pulled a box of Kleenex between them.

They'd need them. Joanna didn't mince words.

"The first miscarriage Jon and I suffered happened three days after I'd taken the pregnancy test. I chalked it up to a false positive and a late period. They found the hormones still present when Jon insisted I go to the doctor."

"Jon and I didn't even get a moment to celebrate, and we know this sort of thing can happen, so we tried again."

Joanna paused her story to burp a sleepy Sara-Jane, buckle her into the swing beside them, and set it to a gentle rocking motion. When she settled back onto her stool, Jess covered Joanna's hand with hers, returning the comfort she'd given minutes ago.

"I am sorry you experienced such a profound loss."

Jo cleared her throat, but the emotional and physical pain she went through remained in her voice. "Our first loss is the least painful, yet no less tragic. It gets worse before it gets better," Joanna said, staring at her sleeping daughter.

"We got pregnant the second time, about four months later, and I didn't tell Jon for two weeks because I wanted to make sure it was real. I even went to the ob-gyn alone. When she confirmed the pregnancy, I even got to hear the tiny flutter of its heartbeat. I told Jon over dinner that night. He laughed and cried, then kissed my belly."

"We lost them at two and a half months. Weeks shy of the appointment for our first ultrasound. We planned to tell Jasper and Jon's parents, but we gave them the news of our loss instead. They shared our grief, and it became an easier burden for us to carry."

Jess clenched her hands together beneath the counter until her nails cut into her skin, and anger and shame consumed her. She abandoned those she loved the most, unaware of how they suffered.

Why? Her and Joanna's situations may be different, but it gave them the same result. And yet, Jess was the one to turn tail and run.

Her reasons seem fucking inconsequential now.

Jess deserved each slash of pain, cutting into her as Joanna revealed the true spectrum of what happened after she left. Her tears came faster. Her friend, no, her sister, went through something unimaginable. What has she done?

Jess can't ever make her absence up to her friend. Or to Jasper.

"Jon and I didn't try again for another year. After copious amounts of therapy, we decided one more time. One more chance, and if it didn't work, we'd explore other options."

Joanna expelled a deep breath. "Jon and I didn't have any problems getting pregnant. It was staying pregnant, however...sorry, this is the worst part," she said in a pained whisper.

"It took six months to get pregnant when we tried for the last time." Joanna glanced at her with a sad smile. "It differed from the get-go. I experienced all this energy and almost no morning sickness, making it to the fourth month without issue.

"At the ultrasound, we found out we were having a boy and kept the news to ourselves for another month, enjoying what we believed to be a healthy pregnancy. When my baby bump became obvious, we let everyone know our secret.

"Jasper couldn't wait to be an uncle. After what Jon and I went through, he wanted to be there for us, showing up to doctor's appointments to wait with us, checking if we needed anything, like every day," she said with a wry chuckle. "You know how Jasper loves to nurture."

They shared a smile about what they both knew to be true. Then Joanna's smile disappeared.

"I wish he'd missed my six-month checkup. He didn't, of course. He wanted to be there and be the first one we showed our latest sonogram."

Jess met Jasper a few years after their parents died, and his role as big brother merged with that of a parental guardian. He always did his best for Joanna, filling the missing roles their parents left behind. "He loves you fiercely, Jo."

"I know. Jasper's the best big brother a girl can ask for."

Joanna grabbed another tissue from the almost-empty box. "I didn't know something was wrong at first. The technician said I didn't consume enough water, offering me a bottle while they stepped out to give me the time to drink it."

"I knew for sure when the doctor came in. Jon did his best to keep me calm, holding my hand tighter and reassuring me everything was okay while the doctor ran the wand over my stomach." Joanna choked on a sob. "It wasn't okay."

"The doctor shut off the machine a few minutes later and schooled her features when she faced us. Yet she couldn't mask all her emotions. Telling us Jackson had passed away, inside me. I wanted to die, too," Joanna said with a shudder.

"It took me a long time to accept it's not my fault, yet I know I'll struggle with it for the rest of my life.

"When the doctor went over our next steps, and explained that there's the option to wait for natural labor, which can take up to two weeks, or they can give me medicine to induce. There's no way I'd be able to wait those two weeks carrying him inside me, so they induced me then and there."

Jess needed to hold her friend, and pulled Joanna into her arms to cry together. "The reality of delivering our baby, whom we'd then have to go home without, was quite the mindfuck."

"I labored for nine hours until I pushed him from my body. The room remained solemn and quiet when they brought Jackson into the world."

Joanna gazed up at her ceiling, blinking to stem the flow of her tears. "The crazy thing is I kept waiting to hear him cry, but the room remained silent until I filled it with my anguished cries.

"We got to hold him. Our tiny, perfect boy. He looked peaceful, like a sleeping angel." She blew her nose and wiped her eyes. Then she picked up a picture from the far counter and handed it over.

"What a precious angel. Jackson's beautiful, Jo."

"Thank you. The doctor and nurses, every one of them, showed us such compassion. They told us while we might not believe it now, we'd appreciate these precious memories of our little boy who wasn't ready for this world."

Jess stared at the beautiful yet sorrowful photo. "I'm sorry for not being there for you, Jonathan, and Jasper. I failed all of you because I believed myself broken and that he deserved better."

When Jess handed the frame back, Joanna set the photo on the counter beside her and pulled the neckline of her shirt to the side, revealing a set of detailed wings with three tiny starbursts underneath her collarbone above her heart.

"After I recovered, Jon and I took a trip to Europe. We stopped in Glasgow to visit West and his tattoo shop. Jon has a matching one, so we always carry our three angel babies." Joanna let go of her shirt collar, and it fell back into place.

"During that trip, we also visited Jon's sister in Switzerland. It's there we learned about the surrogacy agencies in Ukraine and explored the option further."

"We didn't hear rumors of an impending invasion until it was too late." Joanna held tight to Jess's hands. "I'm grateful my brother and West got you both out safe and sound."

Joanna gave her a sad smile and sat back in her seat, letting go of Jess's hand. "You're now one of a handful of people who know the full story, and I told you to let you know it's okay to accept the things we can't change."

Sara-Jane made a funny face, accompanied by a few grunts and gurgles, drawing their attention. "Remember, I got my happy ever after, Jess. Whatever you decide to do, maybe now you'll realize there are many ways to have yours."

Joanna picked up Sara-Jane from the swing. "I'll have to change her soon. This is her 'I'm about to blow the back out of this diaper' face," she said, pointing to her daughter's scrunched-up expression and red cheeks.

Jess seized the moment to take her leave. What Joanna confided wrecked her inside, and she needed time to process. "Sounds like my cue. Thank you for sharing your story with me. I'll always regret not being here for you."

Joanna pulled her into a one-arm hug with Sara-Jane nestled in the other and walked toward the front door. "Please stop apologizing. While you may not have told me, I understand why you left."

Jess opened her mouth to protest. Joanna stopped her. "And I know it's much more than what you said in the note you left my brother."

Her protest dissolved into a cringe. Joanna shrugged, turning to face her in the entryway. "I admit it's not his finest moment when he told me, yet you can't blame him."

"No, I can't."

"I know you wrote what you wrote to stop Jasper from coming after you, but it's not why you left. Tell him the real reason you did, Jess."

"I'm afraid he'll never forgive me." She wanted to confess everything to her friend. After what Joanna confided in her, she deserved to hear the truth, too. "I can't-" Joanna cut her off, covering Jess's mouth with her free hand.

"Excuse the uninvited touch," Joanna said, removing her hand. "But I can't let you tell me what Jasper needs to hear first. He'll forgive you. I'm pretty sure he already has. Jasper loves you, Jess. He never stopped."

Determined not to be ignored any longer, Sara-Jane's cries added to the scent permeating the air. Joanna patted her back and cooed, "I know, baby. Mama's got you."

She met Jess's gaze and laughed. "The situation in her diaper has reached a critical level, and I've got to take care of this."

"No, of course. I...is it alright if I come to visit again soon?"

"You're always welcome. Jasper's not the only one who's missed you."

Jess reached for the doorknob, and Joanna stopped her with the warning of a protective sister. "He's waited a long time for you to come home, never giving up on you. Don't make him wait any longer. It's the one thing I won't forgive."

CHAPTER ELEVEN

Jasper

Why hasn't Jessica come home?

With most of his time taken by the club, he ignored the ghosts when one year turned into two and two into three. After his night of whisky-fueled revelations, Jasper regarded his home with Jessica through a fresh lens. She left everything behind because she planned to return.

With how they found each other in Ukraine, Jasper didn't realize he'd still be waiting.

If Jessica wanted to fix this, she'd be here by now. Wouldn't she? He checked in with West the other day and confirmed Jess remained in London.

Jasper pushed away from his desk, too restless to stare at his computer screen longer. He wanted, no, he needed to admire something else.

He grabbed the portrait hanging on the wall outside his office window on the way to the basement storage room where he kept the others.

Jasper walked past the admin office, staff lounge, and change rooms, checking in with his staff arriving for their shift. He sighed with relief when he reached the locked door, behind which he stored most of his collection of erotic portraits and paintings displayed throughout the club.

Several lined the walls of this room where Jasper selected new pieces to display every few weeks, keeping the artwork fresh and titillating for their clientele. However, the one he hung below the blackout windows of his office was for him.

Jessica may have pursued a career in nursing, but her passion was photography, taking extra classes during school in her spare time. Their union even became her favorite subject. Jess referred to Jasper as her muse, taking photos of them together. Over time, their sessions became more erotic, exploring their desires.

The more personal ones, where their faces are visible, hang in the studio and their bedroom at home. To his knowledge, no one knew these were of him and Jess.

Jasper stopped in front of the portrait hanging on the far wall of the storage room. Jess ruled within the walls of her studio. And Jasper allowed himself to be her pliant subject.

In the picture he stared at now, Jess put him on his knees and made him flex the muscles in his arms and back with her leg flung over his shoulder and his face buried in the juncture of her thighs.

She draped her long, wavy brown hair over her breasts, letting the strands play peek-a-boo with her pierced nipples. Her fingers twisted in Jasper's hair to hold him in place.

The version hanging in their bedroom captured her face, tipped back in the throes of the orgasm he gave her. Jess clicked the remote at the exact moment when she came on his tongue, capturing her ecstasy with precision.

Her control ended the moment Jess exclaimed she'd gotten some great shots. Then he'd haul her to the floor, hike her hips in the air, devour her pussy, and spank her sweet ass until she'd come on his face twice more.

Only when he'd eaten his fill would Jasper hold her down and fucked her. Hard. One hand wrapped around her neck like her favorite necklace, the other gripping her hip hard enough to bruise, while she came one more time on his cock, and he'd fill her with his cum.

Fuck. His dick is hard. Again.

Not that it matters. Jasper wouldn't come until his wife did. "Goddammit Jess, Come back to me."

Jasper shook his head, unsure how he'd move on if she didn't. He tucked the portrait under his arm, locked the door, and returned to the main floor.

When he finished straightening the frame, Kari bounded up beside him. "Hey, boss."

"Hey, yourself." Jasper looked at the woman who appeared on the club's doorstep demanding a job the day after her twenty-first birthday. He didn't hire anyone under twenty-five, yet he found her sass and determination admirable and gave her on the spot.

Kari became indispensable to the club. Her pleasant professionalism put even the most nervous first-timer at ease, and her never-ending wardrobe of wicked fetish gear gave every guest a tantalizing welcome they never forgot.

Kari's also a dear, sweet girl who reminded him of Joanna. She and her darling little sister Izzy join them almost every week for Sunday brunch. When Joanna revealed she and Jon suffered the loss of their second pregnancy, Kari offered the love and support his sister needed.

During those heartbreaking times, Jasper cursed Jess's absence the most, knowing how much Joanna needed her. How much he needed her.

Jasper eyed Kari up and down, finding her still dressed in her t-shirt, jean shorts, and Doc Martin's with less than two hours until opening.

Why hasn't she gotten ready for her shift yet? Without makeup, Kari looked too much like the vulnerable girl he met.

"What's wrong?" he asked, giving Kari his full attention.

She bit her lip, and tears shimmered in her eyes. Jasper immediately pulled her into a fierce hug and growled, "Tell me who I need to kill."

Kari snorted against his shirtfront and mumbled, "Kind of hard to do when they're already dead. These are tears of relief."

Jasper pulled back enough to catch her gaze. "What are you talking about?"

"The guy who murdered Spencer, the cops found his body in the East River a few days ago."

"Well, fuck."

It took Kari a few months to trust him enough to confide why she sought salvation within the walls of his club. She packed a lot of life into her twenty-odd years. Almost more than he has, and he's basically twice her age.

A teen model, Kari walked the top runways in New York, Paris, and Milan, living with minimal supervision and growing up too fast. She left the industry at nineteen and returned home because her mother abandoned her kid sister with the neighbor.

Kari became Izzy's guardian, and while she earned a lot during her modeling years, it wasn't enough to support them and give her sister everything she needed.

With few options, Kari took a job dancing burlesque. The place didn't have the best reputation, and the boss looked the other way, ignoring the legalities of hiring someone underage amongst his other shady dealings. Naïve to the danger, Kari didn't think she had a choice.

Then Kari fell for the charms of their head of security, a guy named Spencer Cameron, becoming trapped in a relationship with a guy associated with some shady people. More dangerous than Kari realized.

Fearful she ventured down the same dark path her mother took, Kari ended their toxic relationship.

Spencer tried different tactics to lure her back, telling Kari she'd left some stuff behind and to come get it. The night she went to get her belongings, some piece of shit Spencer double-crossed came looking for him. They fought inside his apartment, and weapons got pulled.

Her ex was a piece of shit, but he did Kari a solid, telling her to hide in his bedroom closet when the guy pounded on his door. If he didn't, Kari might've died, too.

From her vantage point, Kari witnessed everything, and when the gun went off, Spencer dropped to the floor, and the other guy fled the scene.

Frozen with fear, Kari dialed 9-1-1. The operator heard her frantic breathing and helped her remain calm until the police arrived. The lead detective found her still hiding in the closet with her phone pressed to her ear.

Kari told the police everything once she'd gotten over the shock. They showed her mug shots, and she identified her ex's assailant. A guy by the name of Leo Freedman.

They put out a warrant for his arrest, and the guy disappeared until the cops found him floating in the East River two days ago.

"The detective informed me with Leo dead, the case is closed. No coming forward to be a witness on the stand, exposing my identity to whomever this Leo guy worked for."

"You know I'd let nothing happen to you. Your place has top-notch security, and you and Izzy are safe. It's not like when you first worked for me."

"Izzy and I are forever grateful. I can never thank you enough for the stability you've given us.

"It's weird, you know? The detective told me I can move on with my life now. It's a strange thing to say to someone, right? My life came to a halt eighteen months ago, yet it didn't."

"You went into survival mode, Kari. You work, then you go home and take care of Izzy. It's not living. It's existing. When did you last go on a date, dance, or play?"

"Nineteen months ago," she whispered.

"Isn't it time you let yourself live again?"

A sassy spark replaced the tears in Kari's eyes. "Why? Do you have someone in mind, oh great matchmaking god?"

"Fuck, your bratty ass needs a Daddy."

"If this person is Jasper Jones approved, you may convince me to meet him."

Jasper laughed. West's going to fall hard for this woman. "I may have someone in mind. If he ever gets his ass back to the city, you'll be the first to know."

"Hmm, if he does, I'll consider it."

Jasper cupped Kari's cheek, all teasing aside. "You sure you're doing okay?"

"Yeah, I guess. I'm shocked it's all over, and I can stop hiding in plain sight. It might be nice to put myself out there again."

"Good." What sounded like a gasp came from the back hall, and Jasper's concerned gaze went from Kari to the dark-haired beauty covering her mouth across the room.

Jess is here.

Holy fucking shit. Jess is here.

Jess looked at Jasper and Kari, jumping to conclusions he never gave her a reason to make. All the same, she made them, and Jess turned away, darting down the hall the way she came.

Jasper let go of Kari and stepped away from her. "Jessica?" he shouted. "Kari, I'll be right back. If I'm lucky, I'll introduce you to my wife."

"Okay, cool. I'll wait right here, beneath this sexy fucking picture of the two of you...not at all awkward or anything," Kari called after him.

Her taunt made Jasper pause. "No, it's not."

"Bossman, I hate to break it to you, but everyone knows it's you. Now, go fix things with your wife. I can't wait to meet her."

"Brat." God, Kari's perfect for West. Once he straightened this shit with Jess out, he'd convince his friend to come home.

Jess is running from him again. This time, Jasper intended to stop her.

Jasper caught Jessica near the door. He yanked her to a stop and pressed her against the wall, caging her in with his arms on either side of her head.

Beyond that, he didn't touch her, choosing to wait her out. When she still didn't meet his gaze, Jasper demanded, "Look at me, Jess."

CHAPTER TWELVE

Jess

Jess spent another night in her childhood bedroom, processing everything Joanna told her. It's way past the time she told her husband the truth.

She asked the taxi driver to stop a block from the brownstone the following afternoon, wanting to walk the last bit and burn off her excess energy. Jess loved this area. Did from the moment she and Jasper toured the brownstone with their agent.

Jasper wanted something close to Joanna without being in each other's back pockets, and the four blocks separating their homes kept the siblings happy.

Mature trees lined the quiet street, and the historic buildings saved from demolition are now beautiful homes. The perfect place to raise a family.

Jessica's steps slowed the closer she got. She still didn't know what to say or do once she reached the driveway and found a black SUV parked there. *Good, Jasper hasn't left for the club.* Jess hopped onto the first step with a 'here goes nothing' attitude.

"Jessica?"

"What the fuck?" Jess screeched, catching the railing, preventing a fall on her ass. She looked up to find Grayson Matthews holding a box marked BEDROOM, staring back at her. "Gray? You scared the shit out of me."

"Uh, same," he said, setting the box down. "Long time no see, Jess. What are you doing here?"

Jessica caught the defensive tone in Gray's voice and didn't blame him for it. Yet she answered his question with one of her own. "You live here?"

Gray rubbed a hand over the back of his head. "Yes, and no. The farmhouse is all renovated, and I like to spend most of my time there, but Jasper lets me use the basement apartment whenever I work at the club or want to stay in the city."

Jess looked at the boxes, end table, and lamp, ready to load into the back of the SUV. "I don't understand. Are you moving out?"

"I-"

"Babe? Did you bring out the box I left by the door? I need to put these in it." A gorgeous woman with violet hair twisted into a knot came out of the side entrance, waving a stack of books. "Oh, hello," she said warmly when she spotted Jess.

Gray wrapped his arm around the woman, drawing her close. "Addie, this is Jasper's-"

"Jessica." Jess held out her hand, afraid to hear how Gray finished the introduction, and said, "I mean, hi, I'm Jess." Addie's eyes widened a fraction when she took her hand.

"Addie Carter. You must be the reason Jasper gives off such intense...'I'm taken' vibes."

"Um...maybe?" Her gaze landed on the book in Addie's hand, giving her the perfect opening to move past this awkward intro. She didn't recognize the title; she recognized the author. "Are you A.D. Carter?"

A blush heated Addie's cheeks, and Gray gently squeezed her hand. Addie straightened her spine and raised her chin, seeming to gather her confidence. "Yes, I am."

"I did a lot of reading during my downtime and may have read The Professor's Naughty Student more than once."

Jess also used the super spicy read in one of her many attempts to give herself an orgasm. The book didn't work either, but she enjoyed the story. "I looked for more of your books. Is this a new release?"

Addie shared a look with Gray, one full of love and adoration. "It will be, though not for another couple of months. You can have this ARC if you want," she said, holding the book out.

"Arc?" Jess asked, flipping over the book to skim the blurb on the back.

When the leather-clad alpha-hole BDSM club owner falls for....

Well, now, Addie certainly has her attention.

"Oh, sorry, it means advanced reader copy. I did a select printing to give to book reviewers, bloggers, and BookTok influencers. Helps create a little buzz and early reviews. They're for friends, too," she added with a hesitant smile.

"Awesome. Thanks, I can't wait to read this."

"Are you here to see Jasper?"

"Addie...," Gray said with a groan.

"What? It's kind of obvious. He's not here, by the way."

Jess shifted her stance and looked away from Addie's observant gaze. "I figured, or he'd be out here by now. Is he at the club?"

Gray ran his hand through his hair. "Where else? He's pretty much there 24/7 since he returned from getting Sara-Jane. It's his MO. Heard you took care of her until Jasper got there. Mighty good of you."

"It's my job."

"Don't downplay what you did. It's much more, Jess, and you know it."

Addie put a calming hand on Gray's forearm. "Listen, I'll finish packing and let you two chat. It's nice to meet you, Jessica." Addie gave Gray a pointed look, then turned to head back inside.

"You, too," Jess called after her. She liked the other woman and told Gray when the apartment door shut behind her. "She's perfect for you."

Gray laughed. "Funny, Jasper said the same when he set her in my path. I knew within a week of meeting her, Addie's it for me."

"Then why are you moving out of here? You're not leaving the club, are you?"

"No, no. I love the place and have no plans to step away. Addie purchased an apartment in the area. So, are you back for good, Jess, or is this a brief visit?"

Jess cleared her throat. "I hope I'm back for good. Jasper and I need to talk."

"No doubt, you've needed to for a long time."

Ouch. True, but it stung.

"Listen, Jess. I love you like a sister, but, well, fuck it, this needs to be said. You tore Jasper up by walking away the way you did. He's living, but he's not. Understand?"

"Yes. I do." Jess looked at a spot on the lawn, unable to meet Gray's penetrating gaze while guilt consumed her. "I've made one of the biggest mistakes of my life, with good reason...though it doesn't seem like a good reason anymore."

"Jess, if it made you leave Jasper and everyone else behind...your reason must've been good. We all knew how much you loved each other, and if I'm not mistaken, you still love each other."

Jess met his gaze, finding warmth and understanding in his dark eyes, not the judgement she feared.

"Jasper will forgive you, Jess. Well, after he doles out your punishment for making him wait all this time," Gray said with a chuckle, giving Jess's shoulder a nudge.

Gray's teasing words filled her mind with images of a shirtless Jasper. His powerful muscles, slick with sweat, wielding every instrument from his hand to a cane. Reddening and welting her ass and thighs.

The thick ridge of his erection pressed against the zipper of his pants....

Damn it. This is not the time to get turned on.

"Yeah, it might be what we both need."

"Pervert." Gray teased some more before pulling Jess into the hug she needed.

"Takes one to know one," Jess said, hugging him back. She didn't know how to take everyone being this accepting. "I better go. I want to get to the club."

"You want a lift?"

"No, thanks. Traffic's gridlocked this time of day, and I don't want to take you away from what you're doing. I'll catch the train."

Gray looked her over and nodded. "Alright, if you're sure. I'll be at the club for the late shift. I'm glad you're back, Jess, and I hope things work out. We've always wanted the best for both of you."

"Thanks, but before we check this off as the reunion of the century, Jasper has to let me in the front door first."

"Jasper never deactivated your access code, Jess. Your membership and privileges remain current. I'm not kidding when I say he waited for you."

"Thank you. How do you all not..." Jess swallowed hard. "Why don't y'all hate me?"

"None of us hate you, Jess. And I get it. Sometimes, when you run, you don't know how to stop. I meant what I said. We are in your corners, ready to support you, no matter what."

Jess sniffled. "Damn it, Gray. You're the sweetest."

"What can I say? It makes me happy when others are happy. Addie calls it my love language. Now, go get your man, sunshine. It's about time you get your HEA." He tipped his head in the direction Addie went. "Author speak for a happy ever after."

Jessica's sniffles turned into a snort of laughter. "Oh, my god. You're head over heels, aren't you?"

Gray looked around, checking no one lingered nearby, and when he turned back, Jess swore he radiated with happiness. "Yup. I'm going to marry her."

Jess keyed in her code at the staff entrance with shaky fingers. When the light turned green, she tugged the handle hard and almost fell when the door opened easily.

Jess peered down the hall, finding no one there. She checked the time. Jasper's got to be in his office, and he'd get a security alert that Jess used her passcode. She took a deep breath and headed left, keeping to the back part of the club to bring her out by the stairs leading to Jasper's office.

Is Jasper already headed her way? Or is he waiting, allowing her to come to him?

Both possibilities sent ripples of anticipation and desire through her system. Jess went down the hall, nothing stopping her from speaking to Jasper...except the one thing she didn't expect.

Jess paused in the alcove to check for anyone else when she heard the familiar rumble of Jasper's voice. She peered around the corner and froze. He stood at an angle, giving her a perfect view of the literal statuesque goddess standing with him.

Her heart ached when Jasper pulled the woman into his arms and cupped her face while she said something Jess didn't hear, noting the intimacy between them, the kind she didn't know how to decipher. Has Jasper moved on, after all?

No. Jess didn't believe it. Everyone told her Jasper had waited for her all this time.

Jess didn't know what to think. She stepped back, and her foot kicked the bar of a cage built beneath a coffee table.

Mortified at being caught spying, Jess raised her gaze to clash with Jasper's shocked one, and the energy crackling between them was immediate.

Jasper dropped his hand from the other woman's cheek and came toward her. "Jessica?" he asked, needing her to answer. Instead, she fled, and the thud of his heavy footfalls chased after her.

Despite Jessica's inner turmoil, part of her basked in the thrill. The prey to Jasper's predator.

Jasper said something else, but the words didn't penetrate the sound of her pounding heart. His warm breath teased the back of her neck, and she tried to run faster, almost reaching the door when his fingers wrapped around her upper arm. He pressed her against the wall next to the door, leaning on his forearms to cage her in, crowding her yet not touching her.

Jessica kept her eyes on the open collar of his shirt, mesmerized by the rapid beat of his pulse, trying to avoid his gaze because once she met Jasper's hazel eyes...the secret she ran with...the words she avoided saying all this time would spill from her lips.

Jasper's heat and nearness enveloped her. Their breath mingled between them, his gaze boring into her, his patience wearing thin until he used the commanding voice she could never refuse. "Look at me, Jess."

"If I do, you'll know everything."

"My patience is at an end, Jessica. I'm more than ready for the truth."

Jess took a deep breath. This is it. No more running. No more evading the man she loved with every fiber of her being.

Her eyes raised from the pulse at Jasper's throat, trailing over the corded muscles of his neck, his trim beard, full lips, straight nose, and sharp cheekbones until she met those beautiful hazel eyes. Jess blinked, and the words spilled from her lips.

"I can't give you something you want more than anything, and it broke me. I convinced myself to set you free in the hopes you'd file for divorce and find someone better, someone whole. Someone who'll give you everything you always wanted."

"Jess-"

"No, Jasper. You demanded to know, and you have a right to the truth. I can't stop until everything is out in the open."

"You're right, I wanted to know." Jasper brushed a strand of her hair out of her eyes. "Jess, I can't let this go further without telling you. You're not broken. Not in the slightest."

"You may change your mind in a minute."

"Never. I love you, Jess, and I have from the moment I laid eyes on you. I've never stopped."

Jasper can say the most beautiful things. Yet a horrible vision filled Jessica's mind, of him reaching into her chest and pulling out her beating heart while the words she never wanted to say dropped like a bomb between them.

"I can't get pregnant."

CHAPTER THIRTEEN

Jasper

"*I can't get pregnant....*"

How did Jasper ever convince himself he was prepared to hear those words? Because he fucking wasn't. It felt like the floor swallowed him whole, yet he remained steadfast in front of her.

"I know."

Shock filled her expression, and unshed tears turned her eyes into shimmering pools of pain. "What do you mean, you know?"

Fuck. He is fucking this up, and Jess looks ready to bolt.

Jasper leaned his forehead against hers, aligning their noses and connecting their breath. He wanted to hold her tight, but didn't dare. Not yet, because when he did, he never planned to let her go.

"Fuck Jess, I'm not saying this right. I've got you in front of me after all this time, and it's fucking me up.

"When I saw you holding Sara-Jane, I still didn't get it. Not until I walked into our house and looked at those three empty bedrooms on the second floor. And how we...I mean, how I talked about filling them with our children."

"That's not fair, Jas. I wanted children, too, but when nothing happened, I made an appointment with my doctor. After several invasive tests, he informed me the painful and irregular periods I dealt with resulted from undiagnosed endometriosis. And the severe scaring it caused means I can't get pregnant."

Jasper wanted to punch the wall beside them just to give an outlet to the pain coursing through his insides, though he'd never scare Jess like that. All this time they could've shared...the support he could've given her.... He couldn't believe she suffered this burden alone.

"Why didn't you tell me and let me be there for you?" A tear slipped down Jess's cheek, but she wiped it away before he could.

"When I came home that day, you went on and on about Joanna and Jon starting a family and how we should, too. Mere hours after I received the devastating news, we couldn't.

"You pulled me into your arms, excited about becoming an uncle, and then you mentioned how it'd be great if we got pregnant, too, wanting our kids to grow up together." Jess shook her head with dismay, and more tears spilled down her cheeks.

"I didn't know how to break it to you. Not when I didn't know how to face it myself."

Jess's pain gutted Jasper. "Fuck. I failed you, Jess. I drove you away, and you carried this burden alone."

"No. It's not your fault. You didn't push me away. I didn't know how to deal with-"

They jumped apart when a bartender, with arms full of supplies, kicked the stockroom door closed and headed down the hall in the opposite direction. Jasper checked the time. The club opened in forty-five minutes, and the staff was setting up for the night. "We need to finish this conversation, and we need to do it somewhere else."

Jasper held out his hand, needing to touch Jess, but in a way that didn't lead to him fucking her against this wall. He felt confident they'd get to the fucking soon enough.

His wife was back, and now that the truth was out in the open, Jasper planned to do whatever it took to fix things between them.

"Come with me, sweetheart. There's someone I want you to meet. Then I'm taking you to one of the private rooms to finish this...conversation."

Jasper linked their fingers and tugged Jess away from the wall, leading her back the way they came until they reached Kari, right where he left her, standing beneath his and Jessica's portrait.

A rhythmic tapping of her foot relayed Kari's impatience. "Bossman, you know my look takes time to perfect, and the clock is ticking," she said when she spotted them walking toward her.

"Sorry, having a life-changing conversation with my wife takes time," he said, stopping in front of the statuesque pain in the ass he cared for like another sister.

"Oh."

"Yeah, oh." Jasper tugged Jess closer to his side, letting go of her hand to rest his palm on the small of her back. "Kari, this is my wife, Jessica. Jess, this is Kari Davidson, one of our best employees. She and her younger sister Izzy are also part of our extended family."

"I knew you'd be beautiful." Kari gushed, tipping her head toward the blown-up photograph behind her, reminding Jess how Jasper displayed his devotion and obsession with her.

"Me?" Jess exclaimed with a blush, warming her cheeks. "You look like you strutted off a high-end fashion runway." Jasper winced, worried about Kari's reaction.

"Perhaps in another lifetime," she murmured, returning the focus to the present.

"Is it okay if I give you a hug? I'm a hugger and like to ask first in case the other person isn't. I also ramble and have bratty tendencies," Kari said. "I'd tell you my astrological sign, but I don't want to overload you with information about me. I'll save it for the next time we hang."

"Oh my gosh, you're adorable. A hug sounds amazing."

Kari glared at Jasper, and he raised his hands in surrender and understanding. He planned to make sure Jess never doubted him or their love again.

Kari and Jess hugged like they'd known one another all their lives, and when Jess loosened her grip, Kari kept a hold of her and said, "I can use another sister, and I know Sunday brunch will be even more fun with you there. I can't wait to get to know you. I can feel we're going to be great friends."

Jess bit her lip and shared a look with Jasper, and he gave her an encouraging smile, wanting her to get to know the people he now considered a part of their family.

"I hope we will, too," Jess said with a smile before stepping back next to him, pressing closer and telling him with her body that they needed to finish what they started.

Jasper was desperate to get Jess alone, which added a particular urgency to his tone when he said to Kari, "You better hurry and get ready. You don't want to piss your boss off."

"Ha-ha, boss man. I know you're a cinnamon roll beneath all that alpha-stern-ness," Kari said with a wave of her hand, her insightful gaze tracking the way Jessica clung to him. "I take it you'll be...busy for the next while?"

"More like the rest of the night."

Jasper kissed Jess's temple, and she emitted a soft whimper. No doubt Jess knew where he planned to take her to finish this conversation.

Kari snapped into work mode. "I'll get Zane to finish the pre-opening; everyone already has instructions for the night." Kari pulled her phone from her back pocket, adding a note to the list of things she needed to do.

"Thank you. It's why you're my best employee."

"Gee, promise I won't let the compliment go to my head, though I may ask for a raise."

"Consider it done," Jasper said, silencing her. He tugged Jess past Kari to the stairs. "If there are any issues, let Gray or Zane deal with them. Oh, and the dungeon's occupied for the night."

"Well, alright, boss man. Don't let me keep you from having a good time." Kari strode off in the opposite direction while Jasper led Jess up the back stairs, past his office, and down the hall to the private rooms, eager to get her alone.

When they stepped into the anterior room of the dungeon, he locked the door behind them.

Jess turned and reached for him. "Jasper, I-"

"Don't. I'm at my limit of keeping my hands off you, and we're not done talking yet." Arousal and nerves heightened the color of her cheeks when she bit her lip and looked away.

"Eyes on me, Jess."

Jasper's gaze skimmed over her with approval. Jessica's hands clasped at the small of her back, thrusting her breasts out while she stood with her feet shoulder-width apart, her toes pointed outward, appearing at any moment like she'd lower into a perfect plie.

"Fuck. I can't stop looking at you, sweetheart. You're goddamn breathtaking."

Her blush deepened, and her rapid breathing increased while the tension thickened. Jasper wanted to skip to the part where he buried his cock inside her, but he needed a few things clarified first. "Why did it take three weeks?"

His gaze didn't waver while Jess shifted from foot to foot, biting her bottom lip. "Well, what with giving my notice and clearing out the flat I rented, plus my meeting and subsequent exit interview from DWB, it took longer than I expected."

Jess cleared her throat. "Your donation went a long way in easing the sting of my sudden departure. Thank you."

Jasper figured they might tell her about the two hundred and fifty thousand he donated in her name. "After witnessing the conditions you and your co-workers dealt with, I needed to do something."

"It will help a lot."

"I plan to do more."

"Jasper...." Jess said so much by merely uttering his name. Her eyes filled with tears, and she looked away.

"No, Jess." Jasper tipped her chin up with his forefinger and traced his thumb along her bottom lip, tugging it away from her teeth. "Don't do that. It's another way of running away. I'm the only one who gets to brutalize these lips."

Jasper's resolve crumbled. "Fuck it," he muttered. Jess's eyes widened, then dipped closed as he pulled her toward him and sucked her bottom lip into his mouth, licking her tender flesh before he deepened their kiss.

When he pulled away, he stared into her eyes, blown wide with desire. "I can't believe I have you in my arms again, Jess. I swear we're going to figure this out together."

Jasper's urgent need to finish their conversation dissolved. Tonight would not end the way things did in London. "What do you need, sweetheart?"

Jess's body vibrated in his arms, and her voice trembled when she said, "Punish me. I need you to punish me."

Jasper studied her, taking in every reaction, and realized Jess deprived herself of many things during their time apart. Like he'd decided he wanted none of life's pleasures without her. Both of them punished themselves in the wrong way and for the wrong reasons.

Hell of a thing for the owner of a sex club to no longer want sex. Unless it's with his wife.

But Jessica's back. She's in his arms, and Jasper's hard as a fucking rock.

"Don't worry, sweetheart. We will finish our conversation, but right now, there's something else you need, and I'm going to give it to you."

"Please, Jasper."

"Fuck, I've missed the way you beg me. What's your safeword?"

Jess tried to shake her head and pull away. Jasper tightened his grip on her chin, stopping her denial. There's something he needed to confess.

"You used your safeword because it was right for you to do. It's what you're supposed to do when you need things to stop. It's what our dynamic is based on. Love, trust, safety, and consent. Do I wish you'd stayed and talked to me? Every goddamn day, Jess, but I understand now why you didn't."

Jasper pressed his forehead to hers. "I carried your note with me everywhere. An ever-present reminder of how I failed you."

"Jasper...you didn't fail me." Her voice hitched, and tears slipped down her cheeks.

"Yes, sweetheart, I did. You know what I did with that fucking note the night I returned from London?"

"What?" she whispered.

"I burned it."

"You did?"

"Abso-fucking-lutely. It's no more. I swear I'll never hold it against you again."

"Does this mean you want to resume our contract? Our marriage?" Jess asked with a hesitant hitch to her voice.

"I want everything with you, Jess. Our marriage, our D/s contract. Everything. It's one of many conversations we still need to have. There is one stipulation I want to address now, though."

"What is it?"

"You can't use your safeword and run, Jess. Not again. I won't survive it. We stop, we take a breath, and we talk. For this to work, we can't keep vital information from one another again. Deal?"

Jessica expelled a breath and gave him a shaky smile. "Deal."

Jasper kissed her, his hand moving from her chin to the back of her head, tangling in her hair. He fisted the silky strands, yanking her head back, and she moaned with desire.

"Now," he growled. "What's your safeword?"

Jessica's lips parted, and she spoke the word that haunted him for over three years. "Sunflower."

It didn't haunt him anymore.

Jasper smiled. "There's my girl. Promise me you'll use it whenever you need to."

"I promise."

"No more talking." Jasper let go of her hair and took a step back. "Strip. Place your clothes on the chair beside you and present yourself for inspection."

They'd done this so many times in the past. Of all the private rooms, they favored the dungeon most to partake in their wicked games.

Jess loved to be punished, and Jasper loved to punish her. Her inner masochist called to his sadist, and it never failed to heighten the connection between them.

Jessica unbuttoned her light blue blouse and then pulled the hem from the waist of her dark denim jeans. Her shirt landed on the chair, and she dragged her hair over her right shoulder, letting him take in the lines of her tattoos when she turned around.

She unclasped her bra, dangling it from her fingertips until it dropped to join her shirt. Anticipation quickened Jessica's pace, and her jeans, socks, and underwear soon joined the pile.

Jasper removed his shirt and draped it over the back of the chair. Unlike Jessica, the rest of his clothing remained for now. Stepping behind her, Jasper gathered her hair, plaiting it down her back in a neat braid, using one of the disposable hair ties the club stocked.

When he finished, Jess laced her fingers behind her head and widened her stance. Jasper trailed his fingertips down the center of her spine, making her arch beneath his touch.

"Perfection," he praised, circling around her, memorizing every inch of her beautiful body.

"It's been a long time for us both."

Jess's brow furrowed over his confession, and said, "I told you it has for me. But...for real, you haven't?"

"What? You didn't believe me?" He made a tsking noise. "Like I told you in London. Nothing and no one."

Jasper's gaze dipped to the juncture of her thighs, her pussy already dripping with arousal. "Jess, neither one of us will leave this room tonight without coming. Multiple times. I promise you."

Jessica whimpered, "Oh, God."

"Do I need to remind you there's no god here, and it's my name you'll be screaming?"

"I may need a little reminding."

Jasper smirked, enjoying his wife's sass. Then he held the door to the interior of the dungeon open. "Now, be a good girl, and get on your knees, and crawl to me."

He walked backward to the center of the room, never taking his eyes off his gorgeous wife, stopping beyond the chain dangling from the ceiling to wait for her. He relished the way Jess swayed toward him. The jut of her hip, with each slide of her knee, tipped the curve of her delectable ass into the air.

A growl rumbled from deep in his chest, and he adjusted his straining cock behind his zipper. Jess's sweet little tits bounced with each deliberate placement of her palms until she stopped at his feet and sat back on her heels, peering at him from beneath her lashes.

"Show me how wet you are." Jess complied, and a wicked grin lit Jasper's face as he admired her glistening folds. "You're so fucking perfect, sweetheart."

"Stay just like that." Jasper opened the nearest cabinet, selected a pair of lined leather cuffs, and secured them around Jessica's wrists. He pushed a button on the wall and lowered the chain from the ceiling to attach the cuffs. "Time to rise, peaches." He pushed another button, and the chain retracted, helping her to her feet.

"Widen your stance." Jasper didn't take his finger off the button until Jess's arms extended above her head. Satisfied with her position, he stepped into her personal space and tipped her chin up, taking in her blown-out pupils and rosy cheeks. "You good, Jess?"

"So good," she said, tugging on her restraints, testing the binds, and finding herself captive. "Please, Jasper. I need...you."

"I know, baby." He nipped at her lips, then perused another cabinet, selecting several items. Jess whimpered and moaned behind him, letting him know she saw each item he chose. Jasper placed the paddle, crop, flogger, and cane within easy reach.

He never used every item, selecting one or two to send her soaring, but he loved to let her anticipate which ones he'd choose.

Jasper trailed his fingers down her arms, tracing her tattoos until he reached her breasts and tugged on her nipple rings, making Jess cry out his name. He cut off the sound by gripping her throat with his left hand while his right slipped between her thighs.

"Gonna need you to let go, Jess." Jasper looked deep into her eyes and nipped her tender bottom lip. His fingers slid between her slick folds. "I need you to come for me first."

CHAPTER FOURTEEN

Jess

Jess gasped, and Jasper tightened his grip on her throat. His hazel eyes swirled with desire, and his closeness blurred everything beyond his features.

Jasper's words reached her like they traveled down a tunnel to her ears.

"Let go, Jess. No more denial. No more punishing yourself." Two of his fingers slipped inside her while his thumb circled her clit. The pads of his fingers stroked her inner walls, finding her g-spot with a precision he alone possessed.

Their breaths intermingled, and he never took his eyes off hers, working her body into a frenzy she feared she might never reach again. Her core clenched around his fingers. "Yes, sweetheart. I'm fucking right there with you. You're gonna come for me, aren't you?"

Jess swallowed against his hold. For three long years, she tried everything short of finding someone else to make her orgasm. And here's Jasper, setting her off in mere seconds because the chasm she'd built between them finally closed. Her lips parted in a silent scream, and staring deep into Jasper's eyes, Jess shattered into a million pieces.

"Yes," he groaned, then crashed his mouth to hers in a searing kiss, stealing her breath and devouring her cries. The force of her orgasm rattled the chain, keeping her upright.

When Jasper broke their kiss, she shouted his name. Neither of them closed their eyes, not missing a single moment of this epic reunion.

Her voice sounded hoarse to her own ears when she asked, "Did you...?"

Jasper's hand moved from her throat to cup her jaw. A satisfied smirk on his face. "With the way you fell apart in my arms? Damn right, I came in my pants like a randy fucking teenager." He gave Jess a look filled with wicked intent. "And now you're going to clean me up."

Jess tried to press closer, but her restraints kept her in place. "Fuck yes." Jess was desperate to know if he tasted like she remembered. She licked her lips with anticipation and whispered, "Please, Jasper. I need to taste you."

"Patience, sweetheart. I'm going to add some slack to the chain. Get on your knees when I do."

"Yes, Sir." When her ass hovered above her heels, Jasper stopped her descent. Then he wasted no time undoing his pants and pulling his dick out.

He smeared her lips with the cum still dripping from his slit. "Fuck, you're beautiful. Open your mouth, baby, and lick me clean."

Jess parted her lips and sucked the head of his cock into her mouth, swirling her tongue over him and catching every drop of his salty flavor. "Mm," she moaned around him. Fuck, she missed his taste.

When she left, she never believed she'd experience being with Jasper again. And now? Jess never wanted to stop.

She licked every inch of him while Jasper worked his cock in and out of her mouth. He was growing hard and ready for her again when a growl rumbled from deep in his chest. He pulled free from her swollen lips, leaving her bereft and begging for more.

"Another time, sweetheart. The next time I come, it's gonna be while your tight little cunt is milking me dry."

Oh. Fuck. Yes.

Jasper tipped her head up, and she met his gaze with half-lidded eyes while the endorphins from her first orgasm in years coursed through her system.

Jess licked the last of his cum from her lips, watching as Jasper reached over and selected the implement for the punishment she'd denied herself for too long.

Jasper dangled the leather flogger in front of her, teasing the tassels over her skin until they draped against her back. "Is this what you need to earn my cock? You want me to set your skin on fire, then fuck you?"

His thumb caressed her bottom lip while he waited for her answer. Her voice sounded raspy when she begged, "Please."

"What's your safeword?"

This time, Jess didn't hesitate to answer. "Sunflower."

"Yes, sweetheart. Never think twice about using it. Everything will stop, and we'll talk it out. No more running."

"No more running." She promised.

Jasper straightened to his full height, leaving the flogger draped over her back while he tucked his cock back into his boxers. He left his pants undone, sitting low on his hips, showing off his sexy-as-fuck V-taper.

He grasped the flogger's handle, and the leather tassels left goosebumps in their wake as he dragged it from her body and stepped behind her.

"Let me raise you back up. I want you to stand with your feet spread wide when I do. I won't hesitate to put you in a spreader bar if you don't comply."

"Yes, Sir."

"Fuck," Jasper growled against the shell of her ear, "Do you know what those words do to me?"

Jess smiled to herself. She did.

Jasper pulled the chain taut and helped her stand. He pressed his body against hers while she widened her stance to his liking, massaging her ass with one hand while he held the flogger against her hip with the other.

Jess shuddered in his arms when he whispered, "I've missed you. I've missed this. Us."

"Me, too," she said with a sigh.

"You ready?"

"So fucking ready."

Jasper stepped back, and Jess missed the heat of his body. Then the first strike landed between her shoulders, setting her skin ablaze.

"How many are you going to take for me, Jess?" Jasper demanded.

She wanted to shout 'all of them,' but Jess knew her body's limits and answered, "Twenty. May I have twenty? Please, Sir?"

"Are you sure you can handle twenty?"

Her body vibrated with anticipation, and arousal dripped down her inner thighs. "I can take whatever you give me."

"Good girl. Count them for me."

The thud of the next blow landed, and Jess soared as tiny sparks cascaded over her skin. "Two," she cried.

Each hit landed with slow and methodical precision while Jasper moved the flogger down her back, over her ass, and to the backs of her thighs. With each strike, the number tumbled from her lips until she reached twenty, and Jasper let the flogger fall to the floor.

The wave of sensation Jess floated on never diminished. Jasper dropped to his knees and shoved his face between her cheeks, devouring her from behind. "Oh god, Jasper. Don't stop."

"I'm going to give you everything, sweet girl." His words came out muffled with his mouth pressed against her pussy. The vibrations made her core pulse, desperate for his cock.

"Please...." The whipping he gave her brought her close to the edge, and when he sucked her clit into his mouth, she spiraled into another earth-shattering release, crying out Jasper's name over and over.

Jess hung like a limp noodle from her shackles while Jasper pressed kisses up her spine. When he straightened, the heavy weight of his cock brushed her ass, leaving a sticky trail of precum as he guided it to the opening of her pussy.

Jasper wrapped his arm across her chest, and with his face buried against her neck, she heard him whisper, "I love you." Then he thrust inside her, seating himself to the hilt, and everything fell into place.

She'd come home.

The intense fullness made her rise onto the tips of her toes. Fuck. She needed a minute to adjust. Jasper gripped her hips and pressed his forehead against her back, waiting until she was ready. "Tell me when Jess."

"Oh, God. Fuck, now Jasper. Please."

Their heavy breaths and the slapping of their flesh filled the dungeon and echoed off the walls. The grip with which Jasper held her hips promised delicate bruises, marking her and staking his claim.

Jasper slid one hand between her legs while the other glided over her breast, tweaking her nipple, tugging on her piercing until she cried out in ecstasy.

He stroked her clit with his other hand, working her bundle of nerves into a frenzy of sensation which rippled through her core, making Jasper groan as she clenched around him.

"Yes," he hissed, licking the sweat from her nape. "Fuck, you're incredible, Jess. Come for me. Soak my cock in your release, and I'll give you everything I have."

Jasper gripped her throat, slowing her blood flow and restricting her oxygen, working his fingers between her thighs faster while pumping his cock into her.

Jess's body tightened, and then every muscle let go at once. She convulsed in Jasper's arms, pulsing around his engorged cock, screaming his name while the most intense orgasm of her life consumed her.

Jasper followed her seconds later, and his heat filled her, coating the walls of her pussy while he groaned her name against the back of her neck.

They clung to one another, their bodies slick with sweat. Jasper loosened his grip on her throat but didn't release her. His panting breaths teased the hair clinging to her nape while his cock remained deep inside her, twitching in the aftermath of his release.

The silence stretched between them until she broke it with the ultimate question. "What do we do now?"

He stiffened against her, and despite everything happening tonight, Jess braced herself for his rejection.

Then Jasper's body relaxed, and his lips brushed her ear. "I need you near me, Jess. I don't want to let you go, but I know we can't resume our lives like nothing's happened. We both need time to figure all this out."

"I know."

Jasper's cock softened, and he slipped from her body. His cum dripped from her slit, splattering on the floor between her feet.

Despite the heaviness of their words, Jess knew the sight would captivate her husband and arouse him all over again.

"Fuck, that's hot," he groaned, stroking his cock with renewed interest.

"Oh, um...." While Jasper might find the sight of his cum splattering onto the floor exciting, she didn't need to bask in it. Jess giggled, and any lingering tension between them disappeared.

Jasper chuckled and smacked her tender ass. "Give me a sec to admire how fucking hot this visual is, then I'll get you down and cleaned up."

"Yes, Sir."

"Fuck, sweetheart. You're weakening my resolve not to sweep you into my arms and take you home to our bed."

Jess wanted to plead for him to do it, but Jasper was right. They needed to slow down and get to know each other again. It's hard to hold back when everything feels right for the first time in years.

Jasper pulled on his pants, grabbed a washcloth from the adjacent bathroom, and ran it under the warm water. "Here baby, let me get you cleaned up," he said, bending to wipe away their combined release.

When Jasper freed her from the cuffs, her body shivered, and her teeth chattered. They kept this room colder than the others. Part of the dungeon atmosphere and coming down from her blissed-out high made her shivers worse.

"Easy now, I got you." Jasper lowered her arms and rubbed the stiffness from her shoulders. Then he wrapped one arm around her back and the other behind her knees, scooping her into his arms.

Jess moaned and buried her face in the crook of his neck, and Jasper carried her to the anterior room. He sat on the couch, settling her onto his lap and wrapping her in a clean blanket the club provided for aftercare.

Jasper held a bottle of water to her lips. "Drink, baby." He urged her, drawing soothing circles on her back until her shivers subsided.

"Jess?"

"Yeah?"

Jasper touched her cheek, drawing her attention. "There's something I want to run by you, another compromise, if you will."

Jess met his gaze. "What is it?"

"I want you to move into the basement apartment." She shifted on his lap, and doubt reared its ugly head.

"Hear me out. You'll be nearby and safe. You'll have your own space while we navigate this and get to know one another again." He cupped her cheek, and his stare reached the depths of her soul. "I don't want to lose you, Jess.

"I'll spend the rest of my life proving you're all I'll ever need, but if you envision us with children, let's make an appointment with another specialist, and both get tested. If pregnancy isn't in our future, there are other amazing ways to have a family if we choose to. You're not broken, Jess, and neither is this relationship."

Jasper's words gutted her, and Jess sobbed into his chest as she came down from the euphoric high of their reunion. "I'm sorry, Jas, for everything."

Jasper shook his head and thumbed away her tears. "Enough apologizing. You did what you needed to do. Now you need to forgive yourself. You're not broken or less than. You're enough, Jess, and it's time you realized you always will be."

More than anything, she wanted to believe him. While the doubts she harbored tried to consume her, Jasper gave her something back tonight, giving her the courage to take this leap of faith. "Okay. I'll move into the apartment."

She tucked her head beneath his chin and smiled when his lips pressed against her brow. "Do you mind if we sit here until I'm ready to return to my mom's place?"

"We can take all the time you need. I'll drive you to your mom's when you're ready. I promise, it'll be the last night you ever sleep in your childhood bedroom again. I'm coming to get you and your belongings tomorrow afternoon. Rest now, and I'll take you when you're ready."

CHAPTER FIFTEEN

Jasper

J ess tucked her head on his shoulder and rested her hand on his thigh, his hand on top of hers, keeping them connected on the drive to her mother's apartment.

He kept the radio low and didn't miss it when she said, "Tonight was...."

"A revelation?" he asked, finishing when she didn't.

She laughed. "That's one way to describe it." Several minutes passed, and Jasper thought she'd fallen asleep when, out of nowhere, Jess asked, "Do you hate me?"

"Damn it, Jess. You can't ask me something outrageous like that when I'm driving." Jasper spotted an open space ahead and pulled over.

He turned off the engine, undid his seatbelt, and reached for her; cupping Jessica's face in his hands, he stared into her eyes. The light from the street gave Jasper a glimpse of the turbulent emotions in her eyes when he answered her.

"No."

"I love you, Jess, and I'll never stop reminding you of it. When I say you're it for me, I mean.... You. Are. It. For. Me." Punctuating each word with a kiss.

More tears slipped down her cheek, and he caught them with his thumbs. "No more tears tonight, sweetheart." The endorphins ran their course, and his wife was ready to crash. Truth be told, he'd reached his limit, too.

"I hated myself for such a long time. I hurt you and everyone else I love, Jas." Jess hesitated, then met his gaze. "Why don't you hate me?"

Jasper sighed. "Hurt and mad, yes. I never once hated you, even in the darkest days after you left. I might not have understood then, but I get it now." He cupped her face in his palms. "I love you, Jess. There's no one else for me, and I'll never begrudge you the time you needed to deal with something out of your control."

"I'm not sure I've come to terms with it yet, though; finding each other again gives me the courage to try."

Jasper kissed her, then pressed his forehead to hers. "Let me be here for you now. Let me give you the strength and support you need, Jess. We'll make an appointment with a specialist and get a second opinion. Then, we can decide what to do next. You will not cut yourself off from the people who love you. Your self-inflicted punishment ends tonight."

"I-" She shook her head, her nose brushing his. "Okay. When I'm ready to make that appointment, I'll let you know," she whispered.

"Yeah?"

"Yeah," she confirmed louder.

"Alright. Let's get you to your mother's."

With the traffic, it took a while to get to the other side of the city, and when they did, Jasper pulled into a spot in front of her mother's building and shut off the engine.

Jasper undid his seatbelt, and Jess gave him an exasperated look. "The entrance is right there. I'll be fine on my own. Promise."

"True. I'm still walking you to the door and kissing you goodnight."

"Oh."

"Yeah, oh." Jasper stopped their conversation by exiting his side and rounding the car to open her door.

Jess held his gaze for a moment, then took his hand. He pulled her against him, shutting the door behind her, and with his nose at her temple, he breathed in her familiar scent.

Right then and there, he wanted to put Jess back in his car, take her home, and carry her to their bed, where he'd hold her for the rest of the night. The rest of her life, if she'd let him.

For her, he kept those urges at bay.

"Come on." With his hand at the small of her back, he led her up the front steps while she searched for the key at the bottom of her purse.

When Jess pulled it from the depths, he tugged her back into his arms, tipping her chin up with his forefinger. While keeping their gaze connected, Jasper pressed his lips to her cheeks.

Her lids drifted closed when he pressed a kiss to her brow. Jasper then trailed kisses down her nose until he reached her lips and crushed his mouth to hers.

His tongue slipped past her lips, seeking and demanding control. He moved his hands from her face, sinking them into her hair and deepening their kiss.

When a car horn in the distance sounded, it cooled their heated exchange. Jasper pressed his forehead against hers and said, "Text me when you get inside."

She tucked her head beneath his chin and nodded against his neck. "You're going to stay parked here until I do, aren't you?"

He pulled back enough to meet her gaze. "And if you make me wait too long, I'm coming up there to redden your ass. Much to your mother's dismay."

Jess bit her lip, contemplating the possibility. "I'll have to text you from her phone. I need to get a new one. Beware, once she has your number, expect to get random memes sent to you."

"She already has it, and I already do." It's his and Sylvia's unspoken agreement. Out of respect for Jess's use of her safeword, he never asked her mom about Jessica's whereabouts. She sent him memes and jokes, her way of telling him Jess was good. He cherished each one she sent.

"Why am I not surprised?"

"Because I'm set in my ways? Get a good night's sleep and make sure you and your belongings are ready by three tomorrow."

"So bossy."

"It's my best characteristic. I love you, Jess. Sweet dreams." He kissed her lips again, then she unlocked the door and stepped into the lobby. "I'll see you at three," he reiterated.

"Night," she said as the door closed behind her.

Jasper waited while she crossed the lobby to the elevator. He smiled and waved, not moving from the steps until the doors closed.

The notification arrived by the time he settled behind the wheel.

> **Jess's Mom: Ugh. I need to get a phone. This is weird.**

> **Jess's Mom: I'm in the apartment. And to save you another text to my mother's phone, yes, I locked the door behind me.**

Jasper smirked and returned a thumbs-up emoji, not wanting to leave a record of dirty talk on his mother-in-law's phone. He'll add a phone for Jess on his To Do list and get one for her before he picks her up tomorrow.

He scrolled his contacts until his thumb landed on the right one, and ringing spilled from his car speakers.

"Jasper," Martha purred in her lilting British accent the moment she picked up. "To what do I owe the pleasure of this late-night call?"

He winced, noting the clock on his dash ticked closer to one in the morning. Then he remembered how much of a night owl Martha was. "I need a favor."

"A favor involving a hefty sum toward purchasing a private island when I retire?"

Martha Bedford's success in interior design skyrocketed when she began designing adult playrooms for the rich and famous, including the private rooms in his club.

"Like you'll ever retire."

"Touché. What do you need?"

"I need the basement apartment at my brownstone redecorated. Paint, furniture, household items, accessories, the works." He pulled into traffic while he spoke.

"Did you want me to stalk the fridge and pantry, too?" she asked, sarcasm lacing her voice.

"Shit. Groceries. She'll need groceries. I'll have a delivery service take care of it tomorrow morning."

"Are you renting the suite out? Did you want to incorporate the tastes of the person using it or…?"

"Subtle, Martha."

"I'm anything but, and you know it. When do you need this project completed?"

"By tomorrow afternoon."

"I see. Who's moving into the basement apartment, Jasper? Last I heard, Gray used it during shifts at the club." She sounded almost bored with her inquiry, though Jasper knew better.

"I'd say it's none of your business, but I'd be wasting my breath."

"True. Go on, spill it then."

"Gray and Addison purchased a new place and got the keys last week. I'm sure they'll contact you for your services soon."

"They already have."

Jasper gave an exasperated laugh. "Then what's with the twenty questions if you already knew?"

"Curious what you'd say and if you'd tell me who's moving in."

It's not like she won't find out. "Jessica is going to take over the basement apartment. She's back, and…we're working on things."

"Jessica...your estranged wife?"

"Yes, my wife." Emphasis on the *mine* part.

"Hm. Are you sure you want to spend the money required for my services?"

"Yes. You know Jessica's taste, and I want it done right. Why are you making this difficult?"

"I'm not sure why you want to waste your money on something you hope she doesn't use, or at least doesn't for long."

There's no point in denying the truth. "I need it to be Jess's choice, and for now, she's agreed to move into the apartment, giving her a space of her own while keeping her close. I can't lose her again, and I won't fuck this up."

"Good enough for me. I'll work on some color palettes based on what furniture pieces I have in stock. My estimate and sketches will be in your inbox when you wake up. There'll be a crew at your place by ten. Did you need anything else?"

"Don't worry about the sketches or the estimate. I trust your taste, Martha. Thank you."

"You can thank me with the hefty bonus you'll include with my payment."

She's audacious, yet her skills and friendship are invaluable. "Of course. Consider it done."

"Well, I'm going to get to work on the design. Don't worry. I won't go to extremes since it needs to be done in less than a day, and I doubt she'll use it for long. I'm happy for you, Jasper."

Martha disconnected their call without another word, and Jasper pulled into his drive a few minutes later. For the first time in a long time, the prospect of coming home didn't seem hopeless.

CHAPTER SIXTEEN

Jess

Jess nibbled on her thumbnail, nerves getting the best of her while she waited on the steps of her mother's apartment building. Jasper said he'd be there at three, and by two-thirty, her mother hugged her, kissed her cheek, and then shoved her out the door, telling her to wait for him on the stoop.

According to her mother, Jess's nervous energy is causing havoc with her chakras.

The sun glinted off the hood of Jasper's silver Audi when it turned onto her street. Jess stood, grabbing her two bags and suitcase.

"What are you doing?" Jasper demanded when he exited the car and stepped onto the curb to meet her.

Jess gave him a funny look and tried to go around him. "What does it look like I'm doing? I'm getting me and my stuff in your car because I don't want you to get a ticket for being double parked."

"Give me the bags, Jess."

Why did Jasper have to be bossy and demanding? Why did he have to look so fucking good while he did it?

He wore his short-sleeved, white polo shirt, emphasizing his broad shoulders and chest. Jasper's veined arms, covered in a dusting of dark hair, are the definition of forearm porn. Jess wiped the drool from the corner of her mouth when she caught her reflection in his mirrored aviators.

Jasper gave her a knowing smirk. *Damn it.*

"I said, I got it." Jess pulled some fancy footwork and side-stepped around him to toss her stuff in the backseat.

"Why won't you let me take care of you, sweetheart?"

Jess met his gaze, and her fingers stilled on the passenger door handle. "I understand why you want to, and I appreciate it, but I can take care of myself."

Jasper tugged her into his arms. Thank goodness he held her because his next words weakened her knees. "And I'm reminding you, you don't have to anymore."

"Come on, Jas. It's luggage."

"It's more, and you know it."

Yeah, she did. Jess tilted her head back and kissed his lips. "Let's go home."

Jasper pressed his forehead to hers and hugged her to his chest. "Fuck. Home sounds good. Say it again."

"Take me home, Jas."

"Yes," he groaned, making Jess's stomach flutter with renewed heat. With her self-inflicted punishment over, she was more than eager to make up for lost time.

Jess's imagination may have conjured images of Jasper bending her over the hood of his car. He merely gave her a smoldering look, opened her door, and settled her inside. When he got in, Jasper grabbed a bag from the glove compartment and handed it to her.

"What's this?"

"I got you a new phone and set it up for you." She took it out, finding it all ready to go. The lock screen lit up with a picture from their past. Not just any picture. Jess forgot all about being miffed about the new phone.

"Jasper...is this...?"

He cleared his throat, looking more nervous than she'd ever seen him. "The picture we took on our first date? Yeah."

Jess stared, transfixed, at the screen. "Where did you find it?"

"After...after you left, I went through the files on the Cloud and found it in this obscure folder."

He'd taken her to an outdoor movie night in Central Park, bringing a picnic basket he prepared to enjoy on a blanket far from the other moviegoers.

With the sun setting, casting the sky in an orange and pink glow, he took out his phone, pulled her close, and snapped this picture of them. Jess stared at the camera with a bright smile while Jasper stared at her.

How he looked at her then is much like how he looks at her now.

"Why did you...I mean, isn't this assuming...?" She pointed at the screen, unable to finish the question.

Jasper pulled his phone from his pocket and showed her his identical screen. "It's pretty simple, Jess. I fucking love you. This picture captured how I knew you were the one right from the start." He shook his head. "Listen, if it's not the same for you, you don't have to keep it, but I'm done hiding and pretending this isn't how I feel."

"I don't want to hide either." Jess looked back at the picture, her thumb tracing his image until the screen went dark. "I love you, too. Despite my actions to the contrary, I never stopped. I'm scared," she whispered. "Scared, I won't be enough."

Jasper twisted in his seat and cupped her face, pulling her across the center console into his personal space. Jess clasped his wrists, connecting them as he pressed his forehead to hers.

"I'll show you every day you're enough, Jess. You'll never have cause to doubt it."

He trailed kisses across her cheek until he reached her lips, deepening the kiss when Jess parted her lips. Jasper stroked her tongue with his, demanding her submission.

They broke apart when someone honked and cursed them out when they had to maneuver around Jasper's car. "Mm. We better go," she said, sitting back in her seat.

Jasper's gaze raked over her while he adjusted his straining cock. "I'm doing my best to give us both the time we need, but goddamn it, woman, you've got me wound tight."

Jess bit her lip and stared at her phone screen while Jasper maneuvered them back into traffic, studying the old photo. My goodness, she looked young. *Young and in love.*

"By the way, the passcode is my birthday," Jasper said, taking his eyes off the road to capture her gaze. "I figure it's easy for you to remember."

"Haha."

"You still need to set up your face ID and security. At least you can use it now."

"Thanks. But, um, how did you do this without me having to sign the contract and set up a payment plan?"

His hands flexed around the steering wheel. "I never got around to canceling the plan we shared. Made it easy to add a phone and set everything up for you. I didn't want you roaming the city without a way to contact anyone."

"Thanks, I appreciate that, Jas. It's one less thing I need to do. Let me know how much it is, and I'll reimburse you."

"Fuck no. It's not how it was, nor how it will be. My money is your money. I have more now than I'll ever know what to do with. You don't even have to work if you don't want to."

Jessica's brows raised toward her hairline over her husband's audacity. "Jasper Jones," she admonished. "I will not be a kept woman."

He snorted, and she gasped. "Oh, wow. Yeah...I heard it, yet I still said it out loud."

Jasper chuckled. "I know what you're trying to say. And no, I'm not trying to take over your life. Your independence is something I love and admire about you most. Like it or not, you're a wealthy woman with more than one option. I'm just saying you don't have to return to the hospital if you don't want to. I know the shift work took its toll on you, Jess."

It's something she'd been thinking a lot about lately. What's next?

"I don't want to return to the hospital and won't be re-upping with Doctors Without Borders either, dealing with nightmares and sleepless nights since I left Ukraine. Has made me realize I'm not cut out for that type of assignment."

"Jess...."

"It's okay. I am okay. We'll talk if I need to. I promise. Now, getting back to what I'm doing next, do you remember Dr. Spencer?"

"Tonya Spencer? We met her at the kid's picnic your second year at the hospital, right?"

"Damn, you're good." The way Jasper pulled names and facts always amazed her. "She opened a clinic on the Upper East Side last year and said there's a position for me on her staff if I wanted it. The pay and benefits are top-rate, and the schedule is Monday to Thursday, with weekends and holidays off. It's a pretty sweet offer."

"What about pursuing photography? You have such talent. Do you know how often I get asked to be put in touch with the photographer who took the photos displayed at the club? You can make a substantial living from them alone."

"People want me to take their pictures?"

"I'm not exaggerating when I say hundreds of requests over the last few years."

"Wow, I never considered doing it on a professional level."

"You can even go back to school."

"Maybe. There's a lot to consider."

"I know you love being a pediatric RN, and you've helped so many children and families through difficult times. And the work you did with Doctors Without Borders is commendable, too. I just want you to know you have options. Whatever you choose to do, you have my complete support."

Jess bit her lip and looked out the passenger window, focusing on the familiar landscape when they entered their neighborhood. She never considered school and didn't want to do the full-time student thing. Perhaps a couple of classes to brush up on the latest trends in digital media wouldn't hurt. "Whatever I decide, it'll be because I chose it."

"Of course."

"Uh-huh."

When they turned onto their street and the brownstone came into view, Jasper muttered, "Why am I not surprised?"

Jess's jaw dropped. "Am I looking at a pink Bentley?

"Yup. Someone wants to say hello."

"Who?"

"Guess," he said, turning in and parking beside it.

Jess stared at the pink rarity. "There's one person I know who'd drive a car like this. Please tell me you did not get Marta-fucking-Bedford to redecorate the basement apartment."

"Okay, I won't tell you I got Martha-fucking-Bedford to redecorate the apartment because you've already said it." Jasper gave her a smug look before exiting the car to walk around the front and open her door.

"Jasper," she exclaimed when he helped her from the car to stand beside him. "You've got to be one of the main reasons she can afford this car."

"Two."

"What?"

"I'm one of the main reasons she can afford two. She has a matching one in silver."

"Good lord."

"Come on," he said, taking her hand and pulling her toward the side entrance to the basement. "You know she's in there working on some tiny detail to look busy when we arrive."

"I can't believe you spent Martha-level money on me."

Jasper stopped outside the door, tipping her chin until Jess met his gaze. "You mean everything to me, Jess. I love you and will do anything to ensure your happiness, comfort, and security. The inability to do those things for so long...well, be prepared to get used to it real quick."

Jasper lowered his lips close to hers. "I'm going to be heavy-handed when showing you how you make me feel for the foreseeable future. Please don't deny me, sweetheart. Allow me to indulge in my love language."

"Damn it. You know I can't refuse when you use terms like love language."

He kissed the tip of her nose, her cheeks, her jaw. "Let me spoil you, Jess. I've missed being able to." He wrapped his arms around her and tugged her flush against him, giving her lips a smacking kiss.

"Come on, the sooner we say hello to Martha and satisfy her curiosity, the sooner you can get settled." Jasper opened the door and led her down the stairs. They found the top-tier designer straightening a pillow when they walked in.

Jess gasped, taking in the cozy space Martha transformed. The exposed brick wall, a feature of the open living space, complimented the fresh coat of paint in a warm cream on the other walls. She added splashes of color to the space with accent pillows and a burnt orange and blue patterned carpet on the polished hardwood floor.

"Jessica." Martha clasped Jess's arms, bringing her close for a cheeky air kiss. "It's wonderful you're back. Welcome, welcome," she said, squeezing Jess in her arms.

"Thanks, Martha. It's good to be home."

"Well. Do you like it?" Martha asked, spinning around with arms extended, encompassing the open plan. "Not bad for less than twenty-four hours, right? Of course, your husband made it worth my while."

"Of course he did." Jess side-eyed Jasper, who pretended not to notice. "It's gorgeous."

"Once again, you've outdone yourself," Jasper said, running his fingers down her spine to remind Jess of his presence.

Like she could forget.

Martha preened under their praise. "I knew you'd like it. The bedroom has a similar color scheme with more blue and gold accents. I kept the bathroom's white and black subway tile, adding new accessories and linens. Along with the luxurious skincare products, my assistant swears by."

Jess looked into each room while Martha went over the details. The woman took care of everything she'd need and more. "This is amazing, Martha. Thank you."

"Well, I won't keep you, and I hope everything's to your liking, no matter how short your stay here is," Martha said with a wink.

"Martha," Jasper growled, his warning clear.

"Pssh," she harrumphed with a wave of her hand, not intimidated by him. "Don't kid yourselves when what I say is true."

Jess's cheeks reddened, and she busied herself peeking into the kitchen cupboards to find enough food to feed her and an army.

Jasper drew her attention. "How about I escort Martha out and grab your bags?"

"Alright. The apartment is beautiful, Martha. Thank you again. For everything."

Martha pulled Jess in for a crushing hug. "While it's temporary, I believe it's money well spent," Martha whispered. *Ah, yes. Money is Martha's love language.*

"Come on, Jasper, walk me to my car. I know you're eager to have your wife to yourself. Bye, dear."

"Bye, Martha." Without a doubt, Jess knew she'd be the topic of their parting conversation.

Jasper

Martha preceded him upstairs and out the door.

Jasper followed her to the driver's side of her Bentley to open her door, resigned to the fact she'd speak her mind no matter what he said.

Martha stepped in front of the door, cutting him off. "Be gentle with her, Hm? And I don't mean refraining from what you both enjoy in and out of the bedroom."

"Martha."

She ignored the warning in his tone, determined to impart her motherly advice. "I don't know what made her leave. It's none of my business unless she makes it so. She's fragile, though. If I know you, Jasper, you want to pick up where the two of you left off, and you can't. Despite your best efforts to pause time and wait her out, life moved on."

"I know, and I'm trying."

"Of course you are, dear." Martha palmed his cheeks and pulled him down to her level to air kiss each side. "You know your timing to get me to do this last-minute project is impeccable. I'm on a flight to the UK tomorrow for work. Perhaps I'll run into you both at the club when I'm next in the city."

She winked, tapped his cheek, and then allowed him to open her car door. "Thank you for everything, Martha. You're a dear friend. Safe travels, and we'll talk soon."

Jasper stayed there while she backed out of his drive. With one last wave, she drove off, and he went to the back of his vehicle and retrieved Jess's luggage.

Jess

She looked away from the bookshelves when Jasper descended the stairs and set her bags down. "If there's anything not to your liking or something you need, let me know, and I'll have it delivered."

"Jasper, you ordered enough groceries to fill the fridge, freezer, and pantry. The bathroom cupboards contain every kind of cosmetic I might ever need. There's nothing you or Martha overlooked."

Her hands shifted to her hips. "So...did the two of you have a pleasant chat?"

"Martha's always ready to dish out sage advice; she said nothing bad. Promise." Jasper came closer and held out a set of keys for her to take.

"Those two are for the lock and deadbolt. The third one is your house key for upstairs. And here's the alarm code for both," he said, tapping the paper on the counter.

She took it and tucked it into her pocket, disappointed Jasper didn't elaborate further on what Martha said.

"Thanks. Um, did you want to have dinner with me tonight? Since you stocked the kitchen with enough food to feed me for several months, I'm sure I can whip up something edible."

Jasper shoved his hands in his pockets. "I may have gone overboard with your order, figuring we'd eat together. The thing is, I can't tonight. I have to head to the club in an hour."

"Oh, okay. Another time, then." Jess pushed away her hurt. She's being ridiculous. Jasper owned a business. Of course, it required his attention. He can't drop everything because she wants to have dinner with him.

Jasper came around the counter and grasped her elbow, bringing her out of her inner spiral.

"Jess, I want to have dinner with you. In case you didn't hear me, I bought the food for us. I want to share every meal with you for the rest of our lives, but things will get in the way occasionally. Why don't you unpack and settle in tonight? I would've cleared my schedule to spend the evening with you, but I didn't want to pressure you on your first night here."

Dang, she needed to reign in her neediness.

"Don't you dare," Jasper commanded, and Jess squeaked, realizing she said it aloud.

Jasper pressed his lips to her temple, making her shiver. "Does tomorrow night work for you? I have a few meetings during the day and am free after five."

Excitement filled Jess, and her playfulness returned. "Yeah, I can have something thrown together tomorrow evening. Does seven work?"

"If you don't, there are other things I can feast on," he growled next to her ear. And there went her imagination, picturing Jasper with his head between her thighs.

Feasting.

Which then led her to contemplate not cooking anything at all.

CHAPTER SEVENTEEN

Jess

After Jasper left, Jess unpacked her belongings, finding that three bags didn't take long to put away and cooking for one held no appeal, nibbling on cheese, crackers, and grapes while savoring a glass of wine.

She tried to read, and when that didn't work, Jess soaked in the tub, using some of the fancy bath products Martha selected for her. It helped Jess relax to a point, but nothing kept Jasper off of her mind. She lay awake long into the night, unable to drift off until she heard Jasper's car pull into the drive.

After tossing and turning for the hundredth time, Jess leaned against the counter, bleary-eyed and awake, holding her second cup of coffee like a lifeline.

Movement outside the kitchen window drew her attention, and her breath lodged in her throat. Damn, her husband is a snack. How did Jasper look this good in the morning when he couldn't have gotten much more sleep than she had?

He'd dressed all in black, his button-down shirt open at the collar, the sleeves rolled to his elbows. His pants fit his muscular ass and thighs to perfection, and his aviator shades added a touch of sinister mystery when he slid behind the wheel of his silver Audi and backed out of the drive.

Jess released a shuddering sigh. Her thighs clenched of their own volition, and her hips rocked against the counter, seeking some sort of relief and finding none.

Her gaze moved from the empty drive to the keys left on the counter. The set for this apartment and the one meant for the main house. Their house.

The hours between now and their dinner date stretched into an eternity. *What to do, what to do?* Her fingernails tapped the counter, her hand inching closer to the keys.

Is everything how she left it? Her studio, the clothes in their closet?

Jasper told her it was, and she wanted to see for herself. Jess grabbed the keys off the counter and headed up and around to the brownstone's front door. She looked up and down the quiet street, worried a nosy neighbor might believe this was an attempted break-and-enter.

Ugh, she's ridiculous. Her name's on the deed, and she's holding the key, which her sexy husband insisted she have and demanded she use.

Anytime she wanted.

Jess unlocked the door, and the alarm remained silent. Hm...Jasper expected her. Which made Jess smile and roll her eyes at the same time. She took a deep breath, inhaling the familiar scents of home, and closed the door behind her.

She headed toward the stairs, eager to comb through the closet and collect some of her clothes, when she hesitated and changed direction. Nostalgia pulled her down the hall to the back of the house and the room she used for a studio.

She didn't take any photography equipment when she left. Another self-inflicted punishment meant she hadn't picked up a camera in years. Now Jess worried she sucked at it, that her natural talent had withered away. Her hand trembled when she flicked the light switch on. She wanted to prove herself wrong.

"No way," Jess muttered, looking around.

The room looked and smelled clean, not musty, and unused. Jess peeked into the closet Jasper converted into a darkroom, finding new bottles of developing chemicals with a note stuck to the one in front.

I knew you couldn't stay away. Enjoy your space. Love J.

"Predictable, am I?" She snorted. *Yeah, she is.*

Jess smiled at Jasper's thoughtfulness; looking around the studio, she let the memories wash over her. A lot of joy, passion, and sensual exploration took place in this room.

For the first time in a long time, Jess wanted to create. "No time like the present to brush up on my skills."

Jess went to the shelf in the corner where she stored her equipment, her gaze landing on a case on the shelf below where her old Nikon sat.

Dropping to the floor, Jess pulled the heavy case onto her lap. When she opened it, her jaw dropped. "No fucking way.... Did Jasper...?"

Jess's inability to complete a sentence didn't change the fact that a Sony AR7 V and all the fancy optic lenses with it sat on her lap. "Holy shit. There's gotta be ten grand worth of camera equipment in here. I can't believe he did this. When did he do this?"

She found another note taped to the inside of the case. Jessica pulled it free with a shaky hand and flipped it open.

Jess, I know what you'll say, and no, it's not too much. Nothing's too much for you. Besides...imagine the photos you can take of us with this. <winking smiley face> Love J.

P.S. When I left you behind in London, I didn't get a flight out right away and wandered the streets, killing time, and I found myself in front of this fancy camera shop and came home with this. So, unless you plan to hop on a plane to return it...accept the gift, sweetheart. Can't wait until we can put it to good use.

Jess reached for her phone with the urge to text Jasper. Her fingers hovered over the screen. "I'll thank him over dinner tonight."

She poured over the manual for two hours, playing with settings and which high-optic lens worked best until she felt comfortable enough to take some pictures.

Standing, Jess stretched her stiff muscles, then spread a blue drop cloth on the floor, setting up two lights and her tripod, attaching the new camera. She did a few test shots, adjusting the lighting and her position in every couple of pictures, using the remote tucked in her palm to take each shot.

Jess lost track of time, adding a chair and a mirror...shedding her clothing piece by piece until she wore nothing except her black lacy thong. She adjusted the light, casting her face in shadow.

Jess pulled her hair over her right shoulder, covering her breast, and the light reflected off her nipple ring, playing peek-a-boo through the strands. She cupped her other breast with her left hand, lifting it in an offering to the camera lens.

Click.

Her hand slipped down her stomach and beneath the waistband of her thong. Her fingers slipped between her thighs, and Jess found her pussy slick with arousal.

She wanted to make herself come and capture the moment when she did. Maybe send Jasper each image leading up to her release in a lengthy, sexting tease, driving him wild until he arrived home to punish her for teasing him and fuck her until she'd come on his cock over and over again.

Click.

Click.

Click.

Her fingers pressed inside her core, and Jess rubbed the heel of her palm against her clit. She tipped her head back, and a moan escaped her parted lips.

"Fuck. You're beautiful."

Jess froze, dangling on the edge of orgasm. The low rumble of Jasper's words made her shiver...like he reached out and touched her, despite being on the other side of the room.

Is it after five already? She never planned on being caught. Or did she? Isn't it why she left the door to the studio ajar?

"Don't stop on my account, sweetheart." Jasper's voice sounded even deeper.

Desire washed over her, sweeping her away in its wake. Jess moaned, her fingers moving inside her, stroking her g-spot while she circled her clit with her thumb.

Jess met her husband's smoldering gaze in the mirror as Jasper palmed his erection. His beast of a cock, doing its damndest to break free from the confines of his pants.

"Join me?" Yet, to Jess's utter frustration, Jasper stayed put, stroking himself while his gaze raked over her. The hand shoved between her thighs, matching his pace.

"You know what you're asking for?" His full lips emphasized the gravity of his words.

Did she? Yes...yes she fucking did.

Jess slipped deeper into the pull between them and dared, "Why don't you remind me and do it without your shirt? I want to thank you for my gift."

"You like it?"

"Like it? I fucking love it."

Another growl rumbled from the center of Jasper's chest, causing arousal to flood her hand.

Gaze locked on his reflection, she caught the moment Jasper pushed away from the doorframe and prowled toward her, undoing the buttons at his wrists, then attacking the ones at his front. The last three didn't even make it. Jasper ripped his shirt off and tossed it aside.

Jess stood from the chair on shaky legs and pushed it aside. Jasper walked into the frame, his eyes devouring every one of her curves.

Click.

Click.

Click.

"Cup my breasts. Show off your marks of ownership." Jasper did, burying his face against the base of her throat while he ground the thick line of his erection into the cleft of her ass, driving her wild.

Click.

"Let me remind you of the rules," Jasper said with his lips pressed to her racing pulse. "For each direction you give, you'll earn a lick of my belt once I've warmed you up with my hand. Then-" Jasper paused, his tongue tracing the shell of her ear, making her squirm in his grip.

"Mm...oh fuck. Wh-What else will you do?" Jess asked with a hint of frustration when his words trailed off. Jasper pressed his nose into her hair, breathing her in.

Click.

"I'm going to fuck your sweet little ass. You better pray there's lube stashed in here, sweetheart. Otherwise, my spit and your slick will have to be enough to ease my way inside your tight little hole. Gonna give you a cherry red bottom and a cream pie."

Jess gasped at the picture Jasper had created. "Fuck, yes." Her head fell against his shoulder, and she raised her free hand, sinking her fingers into his hair. She arched her back and pushed her breasts further into his palms.

Click.

"Squeeze them. I love how the light catches on the rings." Jasper kept his face against her throat, and his brows lifted, meeting her eyes in the mirror. He sucked at her skin, and the vibration of his chuckle filled her with his wicked intent.

"You want your ass covered in welts and bruises, don't you, wife?" He ceased needing her right breast to wrap his hand around her throat. Without putting pressure on her windpipe, he used his fingers and thumb to squeeze, restricting her blood flow and eliciting a sense of euphoria.

Jess whimpered and shuddered in his grip.

Click.

"Please...."

When the remote dropped from her fingers to the floor beside them, Jasper tightened his grip and walked her toward the club chair. He bent her over the arm, forcing her face into the cushion, then draped his upper body over hers, caging her in.

"What's your safeword?"

"Sunflower."

Jasper bit her lobe and growled, "Good girl." Then he dragged himself off of her, igniting every inch of skin along the way. When he reached the waistband of her thong, he ripped it at the seams, letting the material fall between her spread feet. "Remember, you can stop this at any time. The power is and always was yours, Jess."

The power. Jasper's unwavering love. His devotion. All hers. Rightness settled over Jessica, and she relaxed, ready to accept whatever Jasper planned to gift her. "Always, Sir."

Jasper lifted off of her and spread her cheeks, squeezing her flesh. "Look how needy your pussy is for me. It's dripping with desire. Your wanton cunt will have to wait. I'm taking every one of your holes tonight, and this one's first."

Jasper's spit hit her pucker, and he rubbed it in with his thumb, loosening the tight ring of muscle until she moaned and writhed against the arm of the chair.

Jess shuddered and pushed back against his exploring digit, wanting more. Jasper didn't disappoint, shoving two fingers into her dripping heat while his thumb worked its way inside her ass.

"Yes," she hissed, arching up onto her toes, and her moans turned into a sharp cry when his free hand slapped the curve of her ass.

"Did you have permission to move?"

Jess whimpered, "No, Sir."

"I believe I told you to stay right where I put you, didn't I?" His palm landed against her other cheek. "You must want the sting of my belt."

So fucking much. "Y-yes, Sir."

Jasper pushed his thumb all the way into her backside and curled his fingers inside her pussy, pumping in and out of both holes while he peppered her flesh with spanks, setting her skin on fire and making her dangle on the edge of an intense release.

Then, just as suddenly, Jasper stopped, removing his touch, leaving Jess pulsing, wanton, and empty. "Nooo.... Please don't stop," she begged.

"Not yet. You'll come when my cock's in your ass. Right now, you need my belt more."

"Yes, Jasper, please!"

He undid his black leather belt and pulled it from the loops on his pants, letting it dangle by his side.

"Ten seems like a reasonable number to redden your naughty bottom."

Jess wanted to beg Jasper for more. She also wanted to sit down tomorrow. "Yes, Sir."

Jasper folded the leather in half, tucking the buckle into his fist, ensuring the metal didn't harm her tender skin. He slapped it against his open palm, testing it. Jess shuddered, rocking her hips, begging him with her body.

"I want to hear you count each strike," he demanded, gripping a handful of her hair. He tilted Jess's head back until their gaze connected. "You're also going to thank me for each one." He brought his mouth close to hers. "Aren't you, Jessica?"

"Yes, Sir." Jess extended her tongue and licked his bottom lip, grazing the soft hair of his beard.

Jasper used the grip on her hair to maneuver her head and devour her mouth with his. She swallowed his groan while his tongue tasted and explored every inch of her mouth. Their time in the club's dungeon may have reestablished their bond. Tonight, it's about reconnection and mending it. "Ready?" he asked when their lips parted.

Jess gasped, trying to catch her breath. "Yes, Sir."

"Brace yourself," he said, letting go of her hair, her head dropping back to the cushion. Jess pressed her palms into the material on either side of her head.

She didn't have to wait long when the leather whistled, cutting through the air, and he landed the first strike across the center of both cheeks with perfect precision.

All the air left her body in a whoosh, and she gasped, "One. Thank you, Sir." Two more fell in quick succession, as did her thanks.

Jasper paused, laying his belt across her back, squeezing her aching flesh, and checking in with her. "Are you ready for more?"

Jess hissed and arched beneath him, her clit rubbing against the arm of the chair while her arousal soaked her inner thighs. "Please, Jasper, I need it. Give it to me. Harder."

"Such a little pain slut."

"I'm your needy little pain slut." Jess is his needy little everything.

"Yes, you are." Jasper traced the belt marks he already left, and then he teased her entrance with the tips of his fingers. "I can feel how needy you are, wife."

"Please, Jasper," she begged, daring to wiggle her ass at him.

"Tell you what, I'll give you the rest in quick succession, from the top of your ass down the back of your thighs. Count them off, and then you can thank me at the end. Do you find those terms agreeable?" Jasper asked, lifting the belt and dragging it down her spine.

Jess shuddered beneath the kiss of leather. Emboldened, she said, "Whatever will get your cock inside me the fastest."

CHAPTER EIGHTEEN

Jasper

Not in Jasper's wildest dreams did he expect to come home to this. No, wait, not true. He imagined scenarios like this every fucking day. The truth is the reality is so much fucking sweeter.

"Who do you think you are, making demands like these?"

"I'm your fucking wife," Jess said with absolute certainty, admitting what he yearned to hear for so long.

"You got me there, wife," he said, landing a smack to her tender ass. Then he draped his body over hers, aligning his bare chest along her spine while rocking his pant-covered cock against her dripping slit.

Jasper sucked and nipped at her nape, marking her. Then he growled in her ear, "As you wish," answering with a classic line from the movie they saw on their first date.

Then Jasper peppered her ass with the last seven swats without pause, and by the time he dropped the belt to the floor, Jess bore ten wicked pink welts across her backside.

"Thank you, Sir," Jess gasped while she shuddered and writhed, absorbing the pain and turning it into pleasure.

Desperate to taste her, Jasper dropped to his knees, parted her cheeks, and pressed his mouth to her cunt. He groaned the moment her sweet flavor flooded his tongue. He lapped and sucked on her pussy lips, then focused in on her clit.

"Come for me, sweetheart," Jasper commanded, sucking the swollen bud past his teeth and flicking it with his tongue until Jess screamed his name and flooded his mouth with her release.

Jasper licked her from clit to slit, catching the last pulses of her orgasm. He eased his mouth from her pussy and reached between the seat cushions grabbing the bottle of lube he stashed there. One of the many places he hid some, never wanting to disrupt Jess's pleasure to find some.

"Boy scout," she mumbled, and his deep chuckle echoed around the room.

"There's something beneficial to always being prepared. Isn't there?"

"Yes," she hissed. Jasper popped the cap, drizzling lube between her cheeks. Jess gasped when the cool liquid glided over her sensitive flesh.

Jasper rubbed a soothing circle against her lower back. "Stay with me, sweetheart. I'm about to fuck you senseless." Jess moaned, and her pucker winked, sucking some of the lube inside. "Look at your body prepping itself for me."

Jess rocked her hips, sucking more of the clear liquid inside. "Please, Jasper. I need you."

"Patience, baby." He slid his index finger against her hole, then pushed inside, breaching the tight ring. Jasper pumped his finger in and out, working the lube further inside. He added a second finger, scissoring them, prepping her to take him. "Yes. Fuck yourself onto my fingers and open for me."

Jasper undid his pants and pulled his aching cock free, coating more lube down his length, readying himself for her. Then he pulled his fingers free and pressed the head of his cock to her stretched opening.

"Breathe in and push out, sweetheart. I'm gonna fill you with one stroke." His balls tightened, and his orgasm built at the base of his spine when he slid into her tight heat.

"Fuuuuck," he groaned when he bottomed out and his balls pressed against her soaking cunt. "The way you take my cock like you're made for me, Jess. Because you are."

Jasper stared at where they connected, and he pulled almost all the way out, leaving the head of his cock inside. Her tight ring clenched around him, desperately trying to draw him back in. He kept hold of Jess's hips, stilling her movements.

"Please, Jasper."

He shifted, giving her another inch. "I know you can beg for my cock better than that, sweetheart."

"Please, Jasper. Fuck my ass. Give it to me hard and deep. I need it. I need you. Please."

"Fuck, yes. That's more like it." He thrusts, giving Jess what she begged for, pumping in and out of her. He loosened his hold on her hips, letting her move to meet him stroke for stroke, bringing them both to the brink.

Jasper reached beneath her, thrusting two fingers into her neglected pussy while he ground the heel of his palm against her clit. "You're gonna come for me, aren't you, dirty girl? Gonna show me how much you love my cock filling your ass."

"Yes...yes, I'll show you. Please make me come, Jas."

Jasper curled his fingers, pumping them in and out of her needy pussy, focusing on her g-spot. He increased his pace, fucking her faster with his fingers and his cock.

Jess made a low, keening moan. Her pussy fluttered, clamping around his fingers, and her ass nearly strangled his cock.

"Yes...right there," Jess whimpered. Jasper shifted his thumb over her clit, working it in quick circles until she exploded around him.

The rhythm of his thrusts faltered, his own release working its way from his balls to his shaft. Jasper grunted with the first pulse of his orgasm. "Yes, sweetheart. Milk. My. Cock," he demanded, unloading every drop inside her.

When the last of his cum spilled into her, Jasper collapsed against her, yet careful not to crush Jess with his weight. He cocooned her with his body. After a few minutes, their heart rates calmed, and their breathing slowed. The other side of such an incredible release is just as sweet.

Jess linked her hands with his when he tried to get up, keeping him there. "Give me another minute."

"Okay." He pressed kisses along her nape, chuffing his nose into her soft hair and letting her floral scent flood his senses.

Jess moaned when he slipped from her body.

"Mm...my cum looks fucking amazing, dripping from your stretched little hole." He ran his thumb over her perineum, catching what creamed from her, and pressed it back inside. "Keep it there until I get you upstairs."

"Um, how? There are a lot of steps between here and there."

"Don't worry, I got you." Jess squealed when Jasper flipped her over his shoulder, carrying her fireman style to their third-floor bedroom.

With his arm over her hips to keep her in place, Jess clenched with each step he took. Jasper wanted to keep her on edge and landed a slap on the cheek closest to his head, garnering another squeal from her and a smack to his own ass.

"My sassy wife still wants to play, hm? You're going to pay for it later. I won't forget." Jasper promised with another spank.

He reached their bedroom in record time, entered the attached bathroom, and set Jess on the toilet to take care of necessities.

"Stay there while I draw us a bath."

"Can't we shower? I want to suck you off," she said with desire and the energy of a woman a decade younger than himself.

Jasper stayed silent, eyeballing her reflection in the mirror while he washed his hands. He turned on the water in the tub, adjusted the temperature, and then added some bath salts, and the fragrance of lavender filled the air.

"Aftercare first. I need to hold you and take care of you. Also, this old man needs more than five minutes to recover."

His teeth grazed her ear, and he growled, "When I get you in the shower, all bets are off. I'm going to fuck your pretty little mouth until I come down your throat, and you're going to swallow every drop. Aren't you?"

Despite his protest to the contrary, Jasper's dick perked with renewed interest the moment Jess gasped, "Yes, Sir."

He grabbed a bottle of water from the mini-fridge beneath the counter and removed the lid, offering it to her. "Here, drink this. You're gonna need to stay hydrated. I've still got two holes to fill with my cum. We are nowhere near done, sweetheart."

Jasper didn't take his gaze off her while she tipped her head back and drained the bottle in half a dozen swallows before wiping her mouth with the back of her hand. "Ah," she said with a satisfied expression.

"You demonstrating how you're gonna swallow me down, Jess?" Fuck the recovery time. Jasper's dick is hard already. Jess daring to give him a knowing smirk.

"Why, you little devil." Jasper swooped Jess into his arms, bridal style, to the sounds of her laughter and lowered them into the steaming, fragrant water.

He ignored his baser needs and pressed a kiss to her temple when she settled against his chest. "I love you, Jess."

She tipped her head back, her lips seeking his, and whispered, "I love you, too."

Jasper massaged her aching muscles until she lay content in his arms and the water cooled. He got out first and turned the water on, and now they stood beneath the warmth of the shower, and he finished scrubbing Jess from the top of her head to the tips of her toes. "Sit on the ledge, baby, while I clean up."

He made quick work of his hair and beard, working through the conditioner once he rinsed the suds free. He lathered soap over his chest, his gaze staying on his wife. She squirmed and clenched her thighs, emitting a soft whimper. "Everything okay over there?"

"Mm, never better. I'm enjoying the show," Jess said, biting her bottom lip and wiggling some more.

Jasper worked the lather over his abs, avoiding his groin and thickening cock, soaping his legs and feet.

The military honed his body, and the discipline they instilled kept it at peak performance. At forty years old, he knew he looked fucking good.

"You missed a spot."

Jasper chuckled and reached behind, soaping his ass. "Did I?" he asked, rinsing the conditioner from his hair and the soap from his body, still ignoring his dick. Which got more challenging the longer Jess wiggled in her seat, jiggling those sweet tits of hers.

"Yeah...there's this big, angry-looking rod between your legs, desperate for attention."

"Oh? Desperate for attention, huh?" he asked, amusement lacing his voice. "You want to give it some?"

"MmHm, I do."

"Let me get it nice and clean for you then, baby." He pumped soap into his hands, stilling on his way to his dick when Jess asked.

"May I?"

Jasper stepped toward Jessica until he stood over her, his dick level with her mouth. Fuck, he loved this built-in bench seat. It put Jess at the perfect height to fuck her face.

"You want to clean my cock after I fucked your naughty little asshole?"

"Yes," Jess whispered. "Let me take care of you so I can worship your cock with my mouth."

Jasper transferred the soap to Jess's hands and guided them to his erection, then he planted his palms against the wall above her, giving him an unobstructed view of what she was doing to him.

He groaned, arching into her touch. She stroked his soapy shaft, thumbing his slit while using her other hand to clean his balls with a massaging touch.

"Mm...fuckin' feels good." Ecstasy coursed through him; he'd never get enough of Jess's hands on his body.

"I do like to be thorough," she said, sliding a finger over the sensitive spot behind his balls.

"Yes," he hissed. Jasper let her play for a few minutes, bringing him closer to his release. "Let me rinse off. I'm close and want your lips pressed to my groin when I come down your throat."

Jess shivered and moaned, "Please." Her hand dove between her legs, and Jasper snagged it.

"Uh-uh. No touching until I say. Hands behind your back. Open your mouth and stick out your tongue. I want to admire the hole I'm gonna fuck while I rinse this soap off."

Jess did what he asked, and Jasper ducked beneath the spray, letting the water carry the suds away. He stroked himself while she shook her sweet tits at him with impatience. "Something you want?" he asked, pointing his straining dick toward her parted lips.

Jess extended her tongue further and formed her lips into the perfect O, using her body to beg him. "Such an obedient girl. You want this?" She whimpered when he pressed the tip to her mouth and painted her lips with the precum gathered at his slit.

Jasper rested the head of his cock on her tongue, and he stroked his shaft. He worked some more against her taste buds. "Close your mouth and swallow."

Her lips wrapped around his crown, sucking every bit of precum from his tip, then she swallowed it down with an exuberant moan.

"Fuck. You're gonna make me come already," Jasper groaned, sinking his fingers into her hair. He wrapped the dark locks around his fist.

"Brace yourself, baby." Jasper shifted his hips forward and plunged his cock into the heat of her mouth all the way to the back of her throat. Jess gagged and swallowed around his length as unshed tears turned her eyes into liquid chocolate.

"What do you do if you need me to stop and can't use your words?" he asked while keeping a steady rhythm, sliding in and out of her mouth.

Jess kept her gaze locked on his and slapped his thigh twice.

"Good girl. Now, you're going to swallow everything I give you." She mumbled a 'Yes' around his girth. "You can touch yourself. Finger your needy little clit, peaches. I want you coming the moment I unload down your throat."

He tugged on her hair. "Show me how much your cunt is weeping for my cock."

Jess spread her thighs, revealing her slick pussy. She slid two fingers inside herself, then held those slick digits up for him to see. "Such a dirty, good girl."

Jasper sucked her fingers into his mouth and licked them clean. "Fucking delicious," he growled. "Now do as I say and make yourself come, sweetheart."

Jess whimpered, fingering her needy clit. Jasper held her head between his palms and pumped his cock in and out of her mouth.

Jess opened for him, relaxing in his hold while he took control, pressing further on each stroke until her nose was against his groin, and she swallowed around him. "Come for me, Jess."

The first spurts hit the back of her throat, and she swallowed him down with a moan.

"Fuck yes. Take it. Take it all," Jasper commanded, fucking Jess's mouth. When she swallowed the last of his release, he pulled free and lifted her into his arms, urging her to wrap her legs around his waist while he devoured her mouth in a kiss, tasting himself on her tongue, and he growled with primal satisfaction.

Jasper stepped out of the shower with Jess in his arms. "I don't want to let you go, sweetheart, but I need to dry us off."

"Mm...Jasper." She nestled her face in the crook of his neck.

He cupped her cheek and pressed his forehead to hers. "Fuck, I love the way you say my name." At one time, he worried he'd never hear it again from her lips. Now he hoped Jess never stopped.

Jasper set Jess down on the plush bathmat and grabbed a towel from the warmer, drying her off and then himself with quick efficiency.

He tossed the wet towels in the hamper and scooped Jess into his arms again, exploring her mouth the same way he planned to explore her pussy.

Jess wrapped herself around him like a clinging vine he never wanted to shake off, and he walked them into the bedroom, laying her out in the center of their bed. Jasper wanted to worship every inch of her skin, kissing his way down her body until he reached the apex of her thighs.

Jess spread her legs and dug her fingers into his hair, trying to guide him to her needy cunt. "Patience, love," he whispered against her skin. "We have all night, and I want to get reacquainted with every delectable inch of your body."

She let out a frustrated whimper when he nipped at the sensitive spot behind her knee.

Only once he sucked and nibbled each one of her toes did Jasper kiss his way back up her body. By the time he reached her inner thigh, he tasted her arousal. "Fuck. You're gonna soak my beard in your juices. Aren't you, sweetheart?"

"Make me come, and I'll do my best to give you a reason to take another shower." She dared to wink, and her saucy words turned into a squeal when he gripped the back of her right knee and pushed her leg toward her chest to expose her ass, where he landed a stinging smack.

Jess rocked her hips and begged for more.

"Do you need a little more pain to go with your next orgasm?" Jasper asked, keeping her leg pressed to her chest, ready to give her another swat if it was what she desired.

"Give me one more. Hard enough to leave the perfect handprint. I want to wake in the morning and still find it there."

"You make the sweetest demands. I promise I'll always give you what you need, baby." Jasper struck the roundest part of her ass, and when he pulled away, a perfect handprint bloomed. "You ready to ride my face now?"

"Yes. Oh, fuck yes," Jess cried.

Jasper hooked her knees over his elbows and flipped them over until Jess straddled his head. "Fuck, your cunt looks swollen and juicy. Ready to be fucked. Come here."

He gripped her thighs and pulled her over his face. "Mm...," he groaned, licking every part of her. "Grab the headboard and soak my beard, baby. I want to drown in your cum."

"Oh, fuck," Jess moaned, tilting forward to grab the top of the wooden frame. Then she rocked her pussy from his chin to his nose, using him like her personal sex toy, and he fucking loved it.

Jasper moaned and sucked on her clit, the vibrations hitting her sensitive flesh, and her rocking increased. "Oh, god. I'm close. Right there...don't stop. Please, don't stop," she chanted.

Jasper took a deep breath and pulled her flush against the lower half of his face, cutting off his air. He rubbed his nose against her clit while he tongue-fucked her opening and sucked on her pussy lips.

Jess ground down on his face, and though her thighs made perfect sound barriers, he heard her scream his name loud and clear. Her release flooded his mouth, and he drank her down like a man dying of thirst.

He sucked in a breath when she slumped forward against the headboard. Not giving her any time to recover, he manhandled her until she hovered over his straining dick.

Jasper captured her lips in a searing, messy kiss while pulling her down onto his cock. They swallowed one another's moans, the remnants of Jess's orgasm pulsing around his length.

He flipped them over, and Jess sank her fingers into his hair and locked her legs around his waist. She clung to him, and he fucked into her slow and deep, balancing on his elbows. Jasper cupped her face and stared into her eyes, rocking their bodies together.

"I love you, Jess. Till the day I die and beyond. We are going to make this work. It's you and me forever, no matter what."

She held his gaze, and tears trickled from the corners of her eyes. "I want that more than anything. I love you, too, and I promise I'll never run from you again."

Jasper gave her a penetrating look. "I believe you, baby." He reached a hand between them, finding her clit. He circled it with his thumb while he pressed his fingers into her lower abdomen. "You gonna come with me?"

"Yes," she whimpered. "I'm close." He worked her clit faster. The sounds Jess made and the way her pussy rippled around his dick told him just how close she was.

"Come with me, Jess." Her body tensed beneath him, and she squeezed his cock like a vise. "I'm right there with you," he groaned next to her ear.

"Oh, fuck yes, Jasper," Jess shouted, and he filled her with his cum.

Jasper kissed her jawline and smoothed her damp hair away from her forehead. "Unhook your legs and straighten them for me."

Her muscles trembled when she did what he asked. It allowed him to roll them over until she lay across his chest. He held her tight, keeping himself deep inside her, and Jess moaned, nestling her head beneath his chin. "Don't fall asleep yet, sweetheart."

"I know. I'll get up and go pee in a minute. There's something about your cock holding your cum inside me." She sighed into the darkness.

There's nothing they can do about getting pregnant until Jess is ready to get a second opinion. The fun thing about a breeding kink is that it won't stop either of them from trying.

"If you keep saying things like that, I'm going to fuck another load into you." Jasper's cock twitched inside her, making his point. Jess groaned and snuggled deeper into his arms.

Jasper pressed his lips against the top of her head, breathing in her familiar flowery scent, and broached the subject Joanna pestered him about. "Jess?"

"Hm?"

"Joanna's hosting Sunday brunch and wanted to know if you'll come. Well, more like she demanded I get you there by any means necessary." Jess stiffened in his embrace, and he used humor to ease the fear she still carried.

"She threatened to axe my favorite brunch food if I didn't bring you. Joanna's playing hardball and making cinnamon buns. You know those buns are my weakness." Jess laughed and relaxed against him.

"She misses you, Jess, and wants to spend time with you. Everyone does."

"You're sure?"

"Positive, sweetheart."

"Okay, I'll go."

Jasper cleared his throat. "Speaking of missing you...."

Jess lifted her head from beneath his chin and met his gaze. Jasper studied her face, tucking a wayward lock of hair behind her ear. "What is it?"

"I know you're staying in the apartment while we work things out, but having you in our place, in our bed...I can't, I don't know... no, I know. Jess, I want you in our bed and home, and I don't want to spend another moment apart."

He cupped her face and kissed her. "Tell me you want the same."

"You said you wanted to take this slow. And what about all the money you spent getting Martha to redecorate?" Her fingers sifted through the hair on his chest, and she avoided his gaze. "I've slept there one night, Jasper."

"I don't give a fuck about the money. Do you want to keep sleeping there? Because you can. I'll hate it, but I'll never stop you from doing what's best for you."

Jasper palmed her cheek, and she leaned into his touch. "I don't want to rush you, but every minute we've spent together since you returned isn't enough. I'm a greedy man, Jess, and I want everything."

Jess captured his mouth in a surprising kiss, and when their lips parted, a smile graced hers. "Good, because I'm a greedy woman who doesn't want to run anymore."

CHAPTER NINETEEN

Jess

Without further hesitation, she and Jasper dove headfirst back into their relationship, and Jess lived in bliss. Perhaps it was ignorant bliss because intrusive thoughts continued to plague her.

Will they fall apart again? What happens if she gets more devastating news? Will she be strong enough to stay?

Jasper insists there's nothing to forgive. Yet Jess left everyone and everything behind and stayed away for over three years. How is it this easy to pick up right where they left off and be in a better place now than they were then?

How did everyone she hurt forgive her?

Her nerves kicked in, and no matter what Jasper did to convince her brunch was no big deal, Jess spent an entire day cooking and baking. Now, they needed to drive the four blocks to his sister's.

When she caught her reflection in the side mirror, Jess bit her lip and fiddled with the overflowing food basket, worry etching her features. "Jess, you didn't need to -"

"Yes, I needed to," she snapped, cutting Jasper off. He veered into a spot down the street from their house and turned off the engine.

Oh, shit. Jess overstepped. Yet she still carried on. "What are you doing? We're going to be late."

"And whose sass will be to blame if we are?" Jasper asked, lifting the basket of food from her lap. "Spread your legs," he commanded, placing the basket on the floor between her feet, keeping them apart.

Jasper's gaze raked over her, then he pinched her nipples, tugging them through her top. "Mine," he growled, making her whimper. The sharp bite of pain sent heat coursing through her, and a rush of arousal dampened her underwear.

Jasper let go of her breast and shoved his hand between her legs. "You know," he said while his fingers stroked along the seam of her pants, pressing the material between her folds to rub against her clit. "I believe you've forgotten the rules, and it's time for a little reminder."

He slid his left hand around her throat, and Jess gasped. She glanced up and down the street. "Jasper, please." She didn't know if she begged him to stop or to keep going.

But when he asked, "What's your safeword, Jessica?" There's no doubt she wanted him to keep going.

"Sunflower."

"Are you using it?"

"No."

He gave a satisfied grunt and went to work unbuttoning her pants. "Such a good girl. I bet when I slide my fingers beneath your panties, I'll find you wet and wanting."

"Yes," she hissed, arching into his touch, and his thick fingers dipped beneath the material. The possibility of being discovered vanished. And there lies the truth. Jess trusted Jasper to keep her safe.

He held her gaze and lowered his mouth to hers. The kiss rocked her to her core while his fingers worked her clit, skyrocketing her arousal until she was seconds away from release.

"You're going to come for me right here on our street in broad daylight," he whispered against her lips. A command she'd do anything to obey.

"And why are you going to, sweetheart?" Jasper held her throat a little tighter, restricting her blood flow and sending a rush of adrenaline through her system.

Jess grabbed his wrist, and the fingers between her legs moved faster. "Because I trust you."

"There's my good girl. Come for me, Jess." Her muscles tightened, and her lips parted.

Jasper captured her mouth in another kiss, swallowing her cries until her orgasm subsided. He softened the kiss, and she whimpered when he slid his hand free from between her legs, almost coming again when he shoved those fingers in his mouth, sucking them clean.

"Now, do up your pants, and we'll finish our conversation without the attitude." Jasper gave Jess a wink, started the car, and pulled back onto the street.

Jess righted her clothing and put the basket back onto her lap. She sighed and said, "Joanna shouldn't be responsible for cooking for everyone."

"She doesn't. Jonathan is a formidable sous chef to her bossy head chef; they always make enough for everyone. You went overboard because you needed an outlet for your fear. And that should've been me."

Jasper reached over and loosened Jess's hand from her death grip on the basket, bringing it to his lips to kiss her knuckles.

"Jess, I can tell you a million times no one hates you or holds leaving when you did against you, but you won't understand until you're with them and see it yourself. I love you, and they love you. And those new to you only want to get to know you better."

She sighed. "I hate it when you're right."

Jasper laughed, taking his eyes off the road to glance her way. "Why?"

"Well, for one, I wanted to drown in my panic and anxiety longer." Jess bit her lip as worry buried its claws in her middle. "You're telling me your sister, Jonathan, and Gray aren't even a little angry?"

Jasper squeezed her hand. "No, Jess. Not even a little."

He bumped the basked with their joined hands and chuckled, "You know, you're lucky we eat like we did in the military."

When they pulled into Joanna's drive, Jess worried she and Jasper were the last to arrive.

"It doesn't matter," Jasper said, reading her mind. "If we're first or last, you remember how we do things? Fancy isn't it. We say hello, fill our plates, and join everyone. Don't worry. Okay?"

"Okay."

Jasper gave her a reassuring kiss, which left her breathless. "Wait there," he commanded softly and exited the car.

Jess couldn't help but laugh as he strutted in front of the car, putting on a show to ease her mind. Fuck, she loved him. Leaving Jasper when she did, the way she did, will forever be her biggest regret.

Jasper pulled open the door, his gaze traveling over her before he leaned close and whispered in her ear, "Do you need another lesson, Jess?"

A blush heated her cheeks. "No, I'm good." Jess gave him a smile she hoped didn't look strained.

Jasper lifted the basket from her lap to allow her to get out of the car. "Damn. How did this not crush your legs?"

"Stop it," she said with a laugh. "It's not heavy."

"If you say so," he grunted. "Come on," Jasper said, leading her through the gate to the backdoor. He maneuvered the basket onto his hip and opened the door with his other hand.

"Hey, we're here," Jasper called, going up the short flight of stairs and into the kitchen ahead of her. Jess rounded the top of the stairs as Joanna came in from the dining room to greet them.

"Oh hey, there you are," Joanna said, kissing Jasper's cheek and wrapping Jess in her arms. "Glad you made it. We need more hungry folks to eat all this food." Joanna's eyes widened when she spied the basket Jasper carried.

"Oh...oh, you brought more. Oh, dear. Okay, let me make some room on the counter." Joanna moved platters and dishes over by the fridge to clear a space. "It seems we may have more than we have bellies to fill."

"That would be my bad," Addie said, walking into the kitchen with a mimosa. "Nothing breaks my writer's block like baking." Addie's eyes rounded. "Oh, shit. You brought enough to feed an army, too. Lucky we have several who used to serve."

"I said the same thing. Told you, Jess." Jasper set the food in the space Joanna created. He gave her a pointed stare while he washed his hands, making her heated cheeks burn hotter.

"I don't know, Jas," Gray chimed in from the entrance to the dining room, pulling Addie into his arms. "Our ladies laid down the gauntlet this time, and we may have to surrender."

Jess's eyes darted back and forth, absorbing all the comradery. The genuine laughter and love she'd missed out on. Her gaze met Jasper's, and he gave her a look, asking, 'Are you okay?' She nodded and smiled, becoming more comfortable by the moment.

With her hands on her hips, Joanna asked, "What the fuck are we going to do with all this food?"

"I know of some people who'd appreciate home cooking like this," Kari said, gaining everyone's attention when she entered the kitchen from the other end of the hall. "I'll make a quick call, then fill you in." She returned the way she came to make the call in a quieter part of the house.

Kari returned a few minutes later. "Um, I spoke to Marie, the head counselor where I volunteer, and she said they'd be happy to take the extra food."

"Where is it you volunteer?" Jasper asked.

Kari cleared her throat, seeming to struggle with how much she wanted to reveal. "Lavender House. It's a shelter for women who've faced domestic violence and abuse. It's a safe place for them and their children to get back on their feet. I volunteer there twice a week and have done so for the past year."

"I see."

Jess eyed her husband and knew his two-word answer held a much deeper meaning. Something terrible happened in Kari's past.

Kari cleared her throat. "There are rules. Men not being allowed is one of them, and since none of you ladies have completed a background check, the furthest we can go to make the delivery is the warehouse where they accept donations. Two of the councilors will meet us there."

"Well, I'm in," Addie said.

"Me too," Jess added. Jasper gave her hand a squeeze and a thankful smile.

"Can I come, too?" Izzy asked, bringing the conversation to a halt when she stepped out from behind Kari.

Joanna gave Kari an 'I've got this' look and got eye level with the little girl. "I hoped you'd want to stay here and help me look after Sara-Jane."

"You want my help?" Izzy asked, her luminous brown eyes assessing the situation.

Joanna dropped her voice to a whisper. "Plus, I need someone to help me make sure all these hungry guys save something for the ladies when they return."

Those big brown eyes squinted at the guys. One hand went to her hip, and the other pointed at them. "You better leave some for the ladies, misters."

The guys, bless their hearts, humored the five-year-old's sass, making pinkie promises while trying not to laugh.

Joanna offered Izzy a hug, and the little girl accepted. "Thanks for being such a big help with them. Want to help read a story to Sara-Jane?"

"Yes, please. Can I pick the story?"

"You can. I'm sure Sara-Jane will love the book you choose."

Izzy looked at Kari. "Is it okay if I stay and help, momma?"

Momma? Jess observed the exchange with interest, knowing Izzy was Kari's little sister.

Kari smiled and ran her hand through Izzy's halo of blonde curls. "Of course you can. Addie, Jess, and I will be back in an hour."

"Promise?"

"Promise." They hugged. Izzy took Joanna's outstretched hand and headed to Sara-Janes nursery.

Addie clapped her hands and said, "Alright, let's get these goodies in the car." She'd drive Gray's SUV while Kari sat in the passenger seat, giving directions, and Jess sat in the back with the food.

After Kari told Addie which way to go, she turned around in her seat and explained the situation regarding her younger sister.

"I caught your look when Izzy called me momma."

"Oh, I didn't mean to pry. It just surprised me."

"No worries. I've raised my sister from age two, and sometimes, when she's excited or tired, she calls me momma. It comforts her, and I don't correct it."

Kari gave her a sad smile. "Besides, I'm more of a mother to her than our own. Families come in all versions. You know?"

Jess knew. In fact, it's something she's realized more and more every day. She reached between the seats and squeezed Kari's hand. "Yeah, I do. Listen, if you ever want to talk...."

"Thanks. I appreciate it." Kari looked out the windshield. "Turn right up here." She directed Addie. "Then make a left into the next alley. Marie said she and Lauren will wait for us." Addie pulled in beside a silver Toyota van, and two women got out.

Both wore jeans and t-shirts; while they may have dressed the same, the similarities end there. One was tall and blonde, while the other sported wicked curves and dark hair streaked with silver. Kari hugged the blonde, then the older woman, holding on a little longer and tighter.

"We missed you this week," the woman said to Kari.

"Again, I apologize for missing Thursday's shift. Something unexpected happened, and now I've-"

"Girl, say no more. We'll have some tea and a chat when you're in on Tuesday."

Kari relaxed. "I'll be there." She pulled out of the woman's embrace and gestured to them. "Lauren, Marie, these are my friends Addison and Jessica. They're responsible for most of the goodies we brought you today."

"I'm overjoyed to meet you ladies," Marie said, shaking Addie's hand first. When she turned toward Jess with her hand outstretched, Jess's greeting lay forgotten on her lips when her gaze landed on the thin silver scar running the length of the other woman's cheek.

A memory from her emergency trauma residency filled her mind. On an overnight shift, they brought a woman in with multiple fractures and stab wounds, including a severe laceration to the left side of her face. Her spouse had assaulted the woman, almost killing her that night.

"Um, hi." Jess found her voice and cleared her throat. "Hello, it's a pleasure to meet you." She turned and shook Lauren's hand, hoping she didn't offend Marie by staring.

"Let's get this stuff into your van," Addie said, opening the back of the SUV.

They transferred everything from one vehicle to the other, and while Addie and Kari helped Lauren load everything, Marie approached her side. "You know, I never got to thank you."

"Thank me?" Jess asked, turning to face her.

Marie kept an eye on the others, finishing up. "I remember little from that night, but I'll never forget your kind eyes and reassuring smile."

Marie reached for her hand and squeezed it. "I remember you held my hand and comforted me. You helped save my life, and I've carried your kindness every day since."

Jess blinked back the sudden onslaught of tears. "Is it okay if I hug you?"

"I wanted to ask you the same thing. Come here." Marie pulled Jess into her arms. "Thank you. You gave me the comfort and care I needed."

"I never forgot about you and always wondered if...."

Marie met her gaze and finished for her. "If I'd survived?"

Jess nodded, emotion clogging her throat, leaving her speechless.

"Not only did I survive, but I also thrived. Now, I give other women in similar situations a safe place to get back on their feet. Do you still work at the hospital?"

"No. I specialized in pediatrics and left a few years ago, doing three tours with Doctors Without Borders." Jess met the woman's inquisitive gaze. "I'm at a bit of a crossroads and unsure of what to do next."

"Now, I bet there's a heck of a story between the decision you made to go and the one which made you come back," Marie said, giving her a gentle nudge. "The kind of story shared over a couple of bottles of wine and some good food."

"Too true. If that's an invitation, I may have to take you up on it sometime." They laughed, and a comfortable silence fell between them.

"You know, we can use someone like you."

"I'm sorry, what?"

"Your crossroads problem. If your plans are to stay in nursing, go private. The women and children who pass through our doors need more than the safe place and counseling we provide. Some have physical injuries and don't want them reported or can't afford to go to the hospital for treatment. We can use someone like you." Marie held out her card for Jess to take. "Consider the offer."

"I will." Jess tucked the woman's card in her back pocket.

"Hey. Everything okay?" Kari asked. They finished getting the food in the van and came to join them.

Marie shared a look with her. "Can I tell them about our shared past?"

"Yes, of course," Jess said, giving permission to discuss their connection.

Marie kept hold of her hand and said, "It turns out Jessica and I have already met. She was the nurse on duty in the emergency room the night Harold laid his hands on me for the last time."

"Oh, my god."

"What are the odds?"

They all spoke at once, and Jess became overwhelmed. She didn't know how to deal with attention like this for doing her job.

Marie took sympathy on her. "Yes, it is amazing. And if you ever decide to get overzealous in the kitchen again, we'd love to benefit. And I hope to see you again soon."

Jess wiped a tear from the corner of her eye. "Me too."

"Good. Come on, Lauren, there's lots to do back at the house." They shared more hugs, then parted ways.

Jess remained quiet on the way back to Joanna's, weighing her options with what she wanted most. Addie and Kari talked up front, leaving Jess to ponder what to do.

The guys waited for them to enjoy the rest of brunch together, and with Addie and Kari's encouragement, Jess told them about her fateful meeting with Marie. Jasper kissed her and praised her for being amazing.

Not long after, Jess escaped to the kitchen with the excuse of cleaning up. After loading the last plate into the dishwasher, she tackled the pots in the sink when Jasper wrapped his arms around her and tucked his head next to hers. "Are you finished hiding from the onslaught of praise? Did you have a good day?"

"Almost, and yeah, I did." She leaned into the warmth of his body and kissed his cheek. "Jas?"

"Hm?"

"I need to tell you something." Jess turned in his arms and met his concerned gaze.

"What is it?"

Jess glanced around. Gray and Addie already left to make the drive back to Connecticut. Kari and Jonathan talked in the living room while Joanna and her eager new assistant, Izzy, got Sara-Jane changed after her nap.

"I want to get a second opinion. I mean, I'm ready to get a second opinion about whether I can get pregnant."

Jasper stared at her for thirty seconds — the longest of her life. Then he asked, "You sure?"

Relieved, she said, "Yes. We can't move forward without knowing all the variables. I'll reach out to my contacts at the hospital and get the name of a top fertility doctor."

"When you make the appointment, make it for both of us. If we're going to have all the answers, I'm getting tested, too."

Jess looped her arms around his neck and kissed him. Grateful every day, they'd found one another again. "I love you."

"Love you too, sweetheart."

CHAPTER TWENTY

Jasper

"You bought me a new wardrobe?" With Jess standing on the landing outside their bedroom and him standing two steps below, she loomed over him with her arms crossed. "Jasper Jones, it's too much."

"Nothing is too much for you." Jasper caught her off guard, flipping Jess over his shoulder and carrying her back into their room. She squealed and wiggled in his grasp until he set her in front of their walk-in closet. He turned her to face the door and wrapped her in his arms.

"But Jasper," she sputtered.

"No. Whether you continue your nursing career, return to school, or pursue your photography passion, you need new clothes." He reached around her and grabbed the dress bag hanging from the hook inside the door. "This one's for tonight."

"We're going out?" She reached for the garment bag, but he held it away from her.

"Yes. I'm taking you to Decadent."

"Like we used to?" Jess asked dreamily, dipping into subspace at the thought.

When Decadent opened, he and Jess christened each of the club's private rooms. In those safe spaces, they learned and defined their wants and needs.

Is she thinking about those nights? Or the times he claimed her in front of patrons who liked to watch? Which did she want to partake in tonight?

"Do you want to add some fresh memories to the old ones?"

"Mm...yes."

"Then that's exactly what we'll do." Jasper kept the garment bag out of reach and looped his other arm around Jess's waist, kissing the sensitive spot below her ear. "I'm going to lay this on the bed for you, then I'm going to draw you a bath, and by the time you finish, there'll be a stylist waiting to do your hair and makeup."

"Jasper...," she whispered, meeting his gaze. "Thank you."

While the stylist pampered his wife, Jasper got ready in the basement apartment. He'd gone for a black-on-black look. Black shirt, black suit, black shoes. He smirked to himself. Black boxer briefs, too. Jessica would look breathtaking in the dress he chose for her, and he'd be her perfect backdrop.

Jasper returned upstairs, saw the stylist out, and headed to their bedroom. A minute later, Jessica appeared in the bathroom doorway, adjusting the backing to her earring, and words failed him as he took in Jess wearing the silvery-shear dress.

When Jess caught him staring, her hands dropped to her sides, and she gave him a radiant smile. "Thank you for the dress. It's beautiful. It...uh, doesn't leave much to the imagination, though."

Jasper's gaze raked over every dip and curve of her body the sheer material teased him with. "Turn around." His voice sounded rough and raspy to his own ears when he growled the command, and Jess spun in a slow circle, showing him everything.

The halter neckline's deep V and how the back dipped to Jess's tailbone displayed her tattoos in exquisite detail. Her stylist twisted Jess's hair into a high ponytail, making her makeup sultry and giving her smoky eyes and siren-red lips. Jasper wanted the color staining the base of his cock by the end of the night.

The lack of material between her breasts framed her cleavage, and the gold chain connected to each of her nipple rings. It's the only other item Jasper left out for her to wear.

"Fuck, Jess. You're so goddamn beautiful."

"Thank you. You're sure it's not too much, or, um, too little?"

How did Jess manage confidence and insecurity all at once?

"It's perfect. You're perfect, Jess."

Jasper strode toward her, picking up her strappy Louboutins on his way. When he reached her, Jasper dropped to one knee and gave her a gentle command. "Hold on to me."

Jess did, and he leaned closer, breathing in her arousal. Fuck, she smelled divine. He held the back of her ankle and placed her foot into the shoe. The straps, adorned in silver studs, gave the illusion of delicate chains wrapping around the arch of her foot to buckle at her ankle. Then he gave the same treatment to her right foot.

When Jasper stood, the six-inch heels aligned Jess's lips with his. "You take my breath away," he whispered against them, wanting to ravage her mouth but not wanting to smear her beautiful gloss.

Not yet.

He pressed a kiss to each shoulder, catching her shiver of anticipation when he trailed his fingers down her throat.

"Ready, love?" Offering his arm for her to take.

Jess met his eyes and smiled. "Yes." She slid her fingers into the crook of his elbow, and he escorted her down the stairs, ensuring her dress didn't get caught on her towering heels.

This woman...she'll never have a reason to second guess her decision to give them another chance. "I love you, Jess."

When they reached the main floor, Jess turned and said, "I love you, too. I swear I never stopped."

"Me either. I hope you know it's the truth."

"I do."

"Jess, whatever obstacles we may face, loving you isn't one of them." Jasper held out his hand. "Come on, let's find out what the night has in store for us."

"We're using a limo?" she asked when they stepped outside, and she saw the driver standing in front of the long, dark car.

Jasper waved him off. "I've got it, Sam," he said, opening the door for Jess while their driver got behind the wheel. He followed her into the car, sitting on the bench against the back while Jess settled on the seat to his left.

"Yes, I hired a car service because I knew the moment I saw you in this dress, it'd be impossible to keep my eyes or hands off you, compromising my ability to keep you safe. With a driver, I don't have to worry."

His gaze traveled over her while the car pulled onto the street. With the way she sat, the length of her gown covered her right leg, while her left remained bare from her sexy stiletto all the way to the top of her thigh. Her pussy kept hidden from his view.

Not for long.

Jasper leaned to his left and pressed a button on the panel beside his arm. "Sam?"

"Yes, sir?"

"Roll up the partition, please."

"Yes, sir." The soft hum of it sliding into place filled the crackling air between them.

Jasper pressed the intercom again. "Oh, and Sam?"

"Yes, sir?"

"Drive until I tell you otherwise."

"Yes, sir."

Jess shifted in her seat, and a seductive smile touched her lips. "All this time to get dressed up." She sighed, putting on a performance for him. "We aren't making it to the club, are we?"

Jasper gave her a wicked grin and spread his thighs, making room for where he wanted her. "Get on your knees and open your mouth, peaches. This little game of Jay and Bey is about to shift into high gear."

Jasper shrugged off his suit jacket, laying it beside him on the seat. Then he undid the cuffs of his shirt and rolled the sleeves up to his elbows as Jess parted the skirt of her dress and slipped to her knees.

He groaned when Jess's plump, cherry-colored lips parted, and her tongue extended. She waited, desire and longing in her eyes, while he slowly unbuckled his belt.

Jasper released his button and zipper next. Then, with his gaze locked with hers, he reached into his briefs and pulled his straining cock free. Holding himself at the base, he sat forward and set the crown of his cock on the tip of Jess's tongue.

He slid it back and forth in the growing pool of her saliva; nudging her lips, he mussed her perfect pout, smearing the combination of spit and precum across her cheek, marking her in the basest of ways.

"You're fucking beautiful on your knees like this. I expect a perfect circle of red lipstick ringing the base of my cock by the time I'm finished with your mouth."

"Yes, Sir," Jess whispered, her lips grazing his tip with each word. He groaned with the light, teasing sensation.

He reached the back of her neck with his free hand and tugged the knot holding her dress up. It pooled at her waist, leaving her sweet tits and chained piercings on display.

"Mm...much better. Don't want to mess up your pretty dress, do we?"

"No, Sir," she answered. Jasper cut off her words when he pushed his cock further into her mouth. He fisted her hair and pulled her further down his length until her eyes shimmered with the only tears he liked. He gave Jess a satisfied smile when the first mascara-laced one tracked down her cheek.

Jasper let go of his cock, easing from the heat of her mouth by tugging Jess's hair. He reached for the chain connecting her breasts and pulled, guiding her back down his length until he reached the back of her throat.

"Such a good little cocksucker," he said with a grunt, pushing his tip past the opening of her throat. "Breathe through your nose, baby. Yes," he groaned when her lips formed a perfect circle around his base and her nose pressed against his groin.

Jess sucked and lapped his length while he thrust in and out of her mouth. When his balls drew tight to his body, he pulled from her lips with a resounding pop.

Jasper maneuvered Jess by her hair until she lay face down on the seat she'd occupied and dropped to his knees behind her.

He raked his blunt fingertips up the backs of her thighs, bunching the material of her dress over her hips as he did. He gripped her ass hard enough to leave bruises and spread her apart, exposing her slick-covered thighs and dripping pussy.

"Fuck. Yesss. So fucking wet for me."

"Please, Jasper." Jess arched her back, begging with her body and her words.

"I'll never tire of hearing you beg for me, Jess. Give. Me. More."

"Jasper, I need you. Please, please, please," she chanted.

Jasper tongue fucked her pussy from behind, humming against her slit, licking her from her clit to her asshole and back again, circling her swollen bud. He sucked on her sensitive clit until Jess cried out.

"You're gonna come on my tongue, then you get to come all over my cock, Jess. I want you to mark me with your release. Make me yours." Then Jasper held her in place, and he ravaged her pussy.

"Mine," she echoed.

"Yes, Jess. Yours from the day I met you," he said against her folds. Doubling his efforts, he sucked her clit and slid two fingers inside her. He curled them, adding pressure to her g-spot with each thrust. "Come for me, sweetheart."

Her muscles clenched, spasms rippling through her when she shouted his name. Loud enough, there's little doubt Sam heard her through the partition. Jasper chuckled, and the vibration prolonged her orgasm. Jess rocked against his face, soaking him in her essence as he asked.

"Mm, yes, baby. Fuck, you're beautiful when you come." Jasper needed to be inside her.

Jess knew what he wanted and begged for more. "Please, Jasper...fuck me."

Jasper pressed her upper body flat against the seat, arching her ass in the air. His body thrummed with anticipation when he notched the head of his cock against her pussy.

Her body tried to suck him in, and he'd never deny either of them such pleasure. He rocked forward, filling her to the hilt with one thrust, and they both moaned with ecstasy.

Jasper draped his upper body along her back and entwined his fingers with hers. He sought her mouth, giving her a searing kiss while he drove his cock in and out of her. "Fuck, baby...the grip you have on my cock makes me never want to leave this pussy. I'm not going to last; I need you there with me. It's all for you, Jess. Take it."

The sounds of their skin slapping and Jess's wet pussy filled the back of the car when he slipped a hand beneath her body to slide over her clit. "Come all over my cock, sweetheart."

Jasper rubbed her swollen bud, coaxing her over the edge. "Yes," he encouraged against the shell of her ear when her pussy tightened around him. "That's it. Fuck, yes."

Jess's whimper turned into a wail, tumbling into an intense release, taking him with her. "Fuck, Jess. I love you."

"Oh, god. Jasper, give me everything."

"Take it. It's all for you," Jasper groaned, holding himself deep inside her tight, wet heat while he gave her everything he had.

When their breathing calmed, Jasper tucked himself away and pulled Jess onto his lap, wrapping her in his arms. He kissed the top of her head, and she snuggled into his chest. He breathed in her sweet scent, now mixed with the remnants of their fucking. His favorite smell. The perfect combination of her and him.

"How are you, love? You, okay?"

"MmHm," Jess mumbled, burrowing beneath his chin, making him chuckle.

"Words, Jess. Even if it's a simple yes."

"Yes." She peeked at him from beneath her lashes. "Please tell me we can hire a car again and fuck for hours while driving around the city."

Jasper smiled and settled her back against his chest. "Yeah, we can arrange another night in the back of this car anytime." He sifted his fingers through the length of her ponytail, smoothing the damage he'd caused.

"Are you okay?" she asked him.

"More than okay." They fell silent when it occurred to him, "You know, I don't recall you ever asking me if I'm okay after a scene. Don't get me wrong, I like it. In fact, I like it a lot." Jasper cleared his throat and asked, "Why now?"

Jess sighed against his neck, her warm breath teasing his skin. "Because I used to believe you didn't require it." She shrugged. "I'd know if there's something wrong. You know? I've learned we aren't mind readers, and checking if you're okay is important, too."

"Fuck, I love you. I promise I'll tell you if there is a time when I'm not."

Her voice dropped to a whisper, every word touching his soul. "I promise I'll never run away again. We'll talk, and I won't keep secrets ever again. I love you, and I missed you every day I was gone."

"Missed you, too." Jasper allowed the emotions to settle over them while the stop-and-go traffic rocked them into a comfortable silence.

"Do you still want to stop by the club? I can tell Sam to take us home, though I'd like you to keep me company while I take care of some paperwork. I don't think I want to scene in public tonight."

Jess left the warmth of his embrace and sat back, balancing her hands on his chest, when she met his gaze. "You don't want to? I mean, you wrecked me in the best possible way already, and we don't need to do anything else." She studied his closed expression. "Is there something more to it?"

Jasper took a deep breath and confessed, "I'm not ready to share you in such a way. To be honest, I'm not sure I'm ever going to be again. Since I found you in those tunnels, Jess, this intense possessiveness has overwhelmed me even more than it once did."

"I like your possessiveness. You've always kept it on the right side of an overzealous caveman, and I'm okay with keeping some things just for us." Jess glanced at the closed partition. "We can always put on a show in our own way."

Jasper stared up at her, captivated by the drying mascara tears on her cheeks and lipstick smudged across her chin. All he could think was Jess had never looked more beautiful. He cupped her cheek and stroked her bottom lip with his thumb.

"What about parading you past patrons like this? Dried mascara tears, your mouth looking well fucked all while my cum drips from your cunt and coats thighs beneath your dress."

His cock hardened with the thought.

Jess bit her bottom lip, catching the tip of his thumb with her teeth, and her eyes darkened with renewed desire. "Did you bring my leash?"

Jasper smirked and reached into his jacket pocket, pulling out the thin chain with a leather handle.

"Hold out your hands," he commanded, and Jasper draped the leash over her palms. Jess looked at it with longing while he secured her dress. When done, he clipped the leash in place with a resounding click.

"Fuck. By the time we make it to my office, I'm going to need to fuck you over my desk. The thought of walking you through the club looking freshly fucked has made me fucking hard," Jasper said, gripping his dick through his pants.

"Please, Jasper."

He groaned. "You keep begging, and we won't leave this car." He leaned over and pressed the intercom. "Sam?"

"Yes, sir?"

"You can drop us at Decadent."

"I'll have you there in ten minutes."

"Perfect." He disconnected, pulling Jess in for a kiss. He licked the seam of her lips, demanding entrance to her mouth. When her lips parted, he teased her tongue with his. They moaned, tasting one another. He angled his head and deepened their kiss, getting lost in his wife until the car arrived at the club.

Sam waited outside their door, not opening it until Jasper gave him the signal. He leaned around Jess and opened a storage compartment, removing two masks. "It's masquerade night."

"You know I love masquerade night."

"It's why I brought you this evening." Jasper placed the silver mask outlined in black over the upper half of Jess's face and tied the ribbon, holding it on beneath the base of her ponytail. The mascara-laced tears staining her cheeks blended with her mask. The look was... "Stunning."

Jasper secured his black mask, edged with silver, and once in place, he gave her a rakish smile and asked, "Ready?"

"Yes, Sir."

"Mm, good girl." Jasper pounded his fist twice against the car's roof, and Sam opened the door.

Jasper got out first, holding his hand to help Jess exit the car. When she took it, he tugged on the leash wrapped around his other hand and said, "Come."

CHAPTER TWENTY-ONE

Jess

The gentle tug on the chain sent pleasure pulsing through her body to her core, reigniting the desire Jasper sated. More electricity sparked, and a moan slipped past her lips when he wrapped his fingers around hers, helping her from the car.

Sam held the door for her in stoic silence, giving nothing away of what he may or may not have heard taking place in his backseat.

The heat searing Jess's cheeks remained hidden beneath her mask while her mind whirled with Jasper's declaration. Finding it didn't bother her how he wanted to adjust the limits of their exhibition play.

Like in this instance, heard and not seen.

They'd done public scenes several times, always on masquerade nights. Jess can admit how she enjoyed having eyes on her and others being overcome with desire by the sight of Jasper pleasuring her elicited a special thrill.

Yet they didn't need to fuck in front of others to experience those sensations. Being paraded around with their combined release slicking the inside of her thighs turned Jessica on even more.

It's hers and Jasper's sexy little secret.

"We'll be here a few hours, Sam. I'll text you when we're ready to leave," Jasper said, getting her attention.

"I'll park nearby. Enjoy your evening." Sam dipped his head in a slight bow, then rounded the car and got back behind the wheel, leaving her and Jasper to follow the other patrons into the club.

Jasper dangled her leash between them, eliciting more pleasurable pain. "Ready, sweetheart?"

"Yes, Sir." And like a switch flipped, Jasper stood taller and broader.

His mouth formed a stern line, and he turned, walking toward the steps of the main entrance without another word, expecting her to follow. Jess fell into step behind and to the right of her husband, following him up the steps like the most obedient submissive.

The slight raise of the security guard's brow was his single outward reaction to his boss arriving at the main entrance with a sub on a leash. His mask did nothing to disguise who he was. "Good evening, Mr. Jones." Jess suppressed the hysterical urge to giggle.

"Any issues?" Jasper asked.

"None, sir."

"Good. Come, pet," Jasper commanded, leading her inside.

Several people in various states of dress wearing masks mingled in the lobby. While others headed toward the suites with cozy spaces to talk or decompress. They also contained the lockers, change rooms, and showers. Even a fet-wear shop.

Jasper pulled her to his side. "The moment I get you alone, you're mine," he growled against her ear. She shivered with anticipation, and Jasper held her tighter.

The cue of guests checking in moved, and Jess spied the familiar statuesque woman behind the counter. "Oh, wow. Kari goes all out, doesn't she?"

"Indeed," Jasper agreed when he turned and took in Kari's ensemble for the night. "Her wardrobe budget rivals her salary. However, our patrons love what she wears, and it's well worth the expense."

"She used to be a model, didn't she?"

Jasper hesitated. "Yes, though it's her story to tell. You should ask her about it sometime. The girl has bottled more life experience into her twenty-two years than most folks twice her age."

"I will." Jess wanted to learn more about the woman her husband considered another sister.

Tonight, Kari dressed like the Halle Berry's version of Cat Woman, combining her outfit with a pair of sky-high platform leather boots, adding several inches to her six-foot frame. She oozed a sultry sexual confidence Jessica envied.

"ME-OW," Kari exclaimed when she saw them. "Now, aren't the two of you purr-fect," she added, playing up her role and giving them an honest-to-god purr while her gaze traveled over them. Kari zeroed in on Jess, and a Cheshire grin parted her burgundy-painted lips. "Hmm, if there's a description of rode hard and put away wet and satisfied, it is you, my dear, new friend."

"Kari -" Jess bit her lip to suppress another wayward giggle when Kari interrupted Jasper's impending scolding with a gloved hand to his face, complete with silver talons.

"Save it, boss man. Not even your mask can hide your satisfaction. Did you want me to set aside one of the private rooms?" Kari asked, getting down to business. Her gaze raked over them once more. "Or is it a spot on the main stage you require?"

"Neither," Jasper grumbled, refusing to elaborate further.

"Alright, alright. I get it. You're playing it cool." Kari said, carrying on with her version of poking the bear. Lucky for her, Jasper didn't bite.

"Anything I need to take care of?" he asked.

"Nope." Kari popped the 'P.' Jasper's eye twitched behind his mask while a weird choking sound escaped Jess's lips.

Jasper acknowledged neither.

"Zane is overseeing the private rooms. Gray did the opening shift until Addie arrived twenty minutes ago, and he's no longer on duty. Max has taken over with no reported issues. It's all smooth sailing, I swear."

"Good to hear." Jasper turned to Jess. "Come, pet."

How many more times did her husband need to say the word come until she spontaneously did? Jasper gave another gentle tug to her leash, sending waves of pleasure to her lady bits and causing more of her arousal to dampen her thighs.

"Have a great time, you two. Can't wait for brunch on Sunday," Kari said with glee and a wave of her talon-tipped fingers.

"She's more exasperating than Joanna ever tried to be," Jasper grumbled when the doors closed behind them.

"She knows the ways to drive you mad," Jess teased him, letting the laughter she held escape. He tugged a little harder on her leash, giving her a bite of pain intended to punish, yet it just turned her on more.

"Funny how all the women in my life do," he said, and Jess shivered from how his gaze traveled over her.

"Hey, we do it with the best of intentions." Jess also believed he liked it, no matter how exasperating they may be.

"I know." Jasper turned, and Jess wanted to melt under the smolder.

She followed him down the short hall to the overlook bar and lounge area. The design displayed the grandeur of the club, giving guests their first taste of what Decadent offered.

Jasper stopped at the glass railing, and Jess leaned beside him, taking it all in. "I didn't get the chance to look around last time. The place is thriving."

Warmth spread from her hand up her arm when Jasper slid his large palm over hers. "Everything looks amazing."

"Thank you."

Jessica met his gaze. "It's even more beautiful and vibrant than I remember. I love how all these people get to be happy being themselves. You must be proud of how it's all come together."

"I am. All of us are," Jasper replied, referring to the members of his former military unit who each held a stake in the club.

He pointed out a few of his changes, but the many patrons staring at them distracted Jess.

She leaned closer to her husband and whispered, "We're drawing attention."

Jasper turned and mirrored how she leaned against the railing, raising her hand to his lips. He kissed the center of her palm, and her fingers stroked his bearded jaw, loving how he leaned into her touch. Then his grin turned wicked.

"I believe it has something to do with the fact most of these people have never seen me with anyone." Then he growled next to her ear, "Ever." The dark vow caused Jess to shiver.

Jasper lowered his lips to her ear. "Hear me when I say this, Jess." She bit back a moan when he tipped her chin until her lips almost touched his, and he stared deep into her eyes. "From the moment I saw you, you were it for me. There's no one else. Ever."

"Fuck. You're killing me with your hotness."

"Yeah?" Jasper asked with a chuckle, tugging on her leash until their bodies aligned.

She teased his bottom lip with the tip of her tongue. "Oh, yeah. Can we save the rest of the tour for later and head to your office?"

Jasper smiled against her lips. "You're not trying to get out of going for a stroll, are you, pet? We are going to my office and taking the long way."

Jasper took her by the leash and guided her down the grand staircase, past throngs of people grinding on the dance floor, stopping to greet several members.

Each step, each delay, each curious gaze turned Jess on even more.

It took everything she possessed to keep it together until Jasper locked his office door behind them. He pressed against her back, surrounding her in his heat. The ribbon holding her mask loosened, and he removed it, tossing it onto his desk along with his. "There, much better."

Jess tilted her head and moaned when Jasper buried his face at the base of her throat. His rumbling groan sent a shiver down her spine. The hand holding her leash pressed against her stomach, and he shortened the length, wrapping it around his fist until his hand stopped between her breasts.

"Do you trust me?"

"Yes," she answered without hesitation.

Jasper made a satisfied sound, and the words whispered in her ear made Jess melt. "I want to fuck you against the window overlooking our portrait."

He walked her over and pressed her against it until no space remained between the cool glass, her, and him. "Look at us," Jasper commanded.

Jess stared at the blown-up photo she'd taken of them, loving how their bodies aligned. She remembered playing with shadows and light, revealing bits of flesh while others remained cloaked in darkness during that session.

The sharp sensation of the cold glass meeting her hard nipples roused Jess from her revelry. Jasper undid the halter of her dress, letting it fall to her waist.

He tapped the pane with his knuckles. "Mirrored glass. I'm the only one who gets to see you come undone tonight. And you, Mrs. Jones, you get to enjoy the view I have every day at work. Those photos used to haunt me. Now they remind me I have you to hurry home to."

Jasper unraveled her leash, draping the chain around her neck. "Fuck, I need to taste you."

Jess gasped his name, and he gathered the skirt of her dress, bunching the material around her hips. "Please."

"Spread your legs, sweetheart, and pull those cheeks apart. Show me how wet and messy you are for me."

"Yes, Sir." Her hands left the glass, and Jess reached behind, gripping her quivering flesh in her palms. She pulled her cheeks apart and displayed her dripping cunt for her husband.

Jasper gripped the backs of her thighs, his fingertips leaving more marks, staking his claim everywhere he touched her. His breath teased her puffy folds, and Jess grew desperate for more. "Please taste me, Sir."

Jasper licked a trail up her inner thigh, gathering their release on his tongue. "You taste divine covered in my cum," he hummed against her skin, doing the same thing to her other thigh, turning Jess on more and more.

At last, Jasper shoved his face against her pussy and tongued her core. She leaned into the glass, and her legs shook with the onslaught of pleasure. Her hands landed back on the glass for balance while her husband held her open for his mouth, worshiping her pussy like the way he'd kiss her mouth.

"Jasper...I'm close...please, I need...." Her words trailed off into a series of moans and whimpers. His tongue flicked her clit, and Jess heard Jasper undo his pants to free his cock.

"Don't you dare come until my cock is deep inside you."

"Please hurry." Jess whimpered from the loss of his mouth when Jasper stood, lining himself up with her opening. He filled her until nothing separated them except the clothes they still wore.

Jasper linked their hands together, keeping his body flush with hers; he rocked his hips, sliding his thick, veiny length in and out of her.

The motion rubbed her mound against the glass, teasing her swollen clit. Jess fluttered and clenched around Jasper's cock on the cusp of her orgasm, not letting go without permission.

Jess fought a losing battle, reaching her limit. "Please...please...," she chanted.

Jasper growled in her ear and nipped her jawline; she knew he'd reached his, too. "Right there with you, sweetheart. Come all over my cock, Jess."

His movements got harder and faster. Jess's muscles tightened, then her core rippled around his thrusting length in a desperate attempt to trap him deep inside her.

Jasper's name ripped from her throat, and Jess cried out in ecstasy; arching her back, she shook with the force of her orgasm, and his hot cum filled her pussy.

"Fuck, Jess. The way you grip me...I swear your pussy is my own piece of heaven." Jasper pressed kisses along her neck, holding her close until he softened, slipping from her body. She whimpered from the loss.

"Stay there," he commanded.

Her panting breaths fogged the glass, and her eyes followed her index finger, drawing a little heart in the moisture. Jess snorted. Like she can move, let alone go anywhere.

His deep laughter came from somewhere behind her.

Guess she said the words aloud.

"Those too," Jasper said with a laugh on his way to the washroom in the corner of his office.

"Damn it."

CHAPTER TWENTY-TWO

Jasper

Jess remained where he left her, pressed against the glass, her dress still bunched around her waist, staring at their picture with a wistful look.

When he returned to her, Jasper trailed his fingers down her spine and trailed kisses along her throat. "Are you alright?"

"MmHm...catching my breath."

"Rest, and I'll get you cleaned up."

"Okay," Jess said, sounding a little dazed.

"Turn around for me, sweetheart." When she moved away from the glass, he caught sight of the *impression* she'd left behind. "It's a shame I'll have to clean my window, but I can't have the staff finding that."

Jess's eyes widened, taking in the image on the glass. "Oh. I can clean it," she said, attempting to shift away from him.

Jasper rolled his eyes. "Woman, I'll take care of it later. For now, let me admire it." He held her chin, keeping her still while he wiped the ruined makeup from her face with a warm, wet cloth.

Jess whimpered when he folded the cloth over and moved his hand between her legs. Once he finished, He righted her dress and settled her onto his lap when he sat in his chair.

He removed Jess's stilettos and set them on the floor, massaging her feet while she snuggled beneath his chin with a soft moan.

"Mm... that's nice." Her breathing slowed, and she drifted into a light doze. Jasper wrapped her leash around his left hand and rested it against her hip. Then he pulled the file he needed across his desk with his right.

Finished with the papers, Jasper closed the folder, ready to rouse Jess and head home, when a sharp-knuckled rap gave the briefest warning before the lock disengaged and his door flew open.

A smiling Gray and blushing Addison stood on the other side. "Please come in," Jasper said. "My door's not locked for any reason."

Addie pulled on Gray's hand to no avail and said, "I'm sorry we interrupted. We can go, and I can make an appointment for a more appropriate time."

Jess sat up and gave Jasper a peck on the cheek. "Be nice," she whispered next to his ear. Then she turned to greet them with a radiant smile. "Friends don't need appointments, Addie. What brings you by?" She folded her hands on his desk, using his lap like her very own executive chair, and fuck, Jasper enjoyed it.

The flush on Addison's cheeks spread down her throat, piquing Jasper's interest in what brought them by.

Gray kissed Addie's knuckles and said, "You've got this, baby." It made Jasper happy to have played a part in putting the two of them onto each other's paths.

Addison straightened her spine, and an air of confidence settled around her. "My publisher wants a unique venue for my book launch party. They tossed around hosting it at an adult toy store or a tattoo shop, and when I told Gray, he added his own suggestion. Here."

"It'd be during off hours," Gray added. "We can even invite guests to stay and partake in what we offer."

Jasper traced the tattooed lines along Jess's arm, mulling over the idea. "Those wanting to stay need to go through the vetting process."

Gray gave him a knowing smile while Addie peered at him with hope and excitement.

"We haven't hosted a demonstration night in a while. If your publisher accepts our rules and regulations, you have yourself a location."

"Yesss." Gray punched his fist in the air. "I knew you'd agree, brother."

Addison cleared her throat. "Thank you, Jasper." Her eyes darted to Jessica, then back to him. "Um, I have one other request. It's about the portraits in the club. Specifically, the ones of the two of you."

Jess shifted against him, no doubt reminded of how she'd spent the previous hour staring at one of them while he fucked her senseless.

"What about them?" Jess asked her.

"You're a talented photographer, and I'm quite drawn to them. How you play with shadows, light, and the contours of your bodies, teasing the observer with a taste of what you're doing, is beautiful, sexy, and alluring. The chemistry pouring from the images reminds me of the characters in my book."

"Oh, um, wow. Thank you." Jess tucked herself closer to him, and Jasper tightened his hold on her, giving her strength.

"I'd love to feature them as part of the aesthetic I want to create. Is that something you'd be interested in allowing?" Addie asked.

Jess dipped her head, always overwhelmed with praise like this, and Jasper gave her the push she needed. "I believe we can showcase my wife's talents and yours." The way Jess leaned into him confirmed Jasper said the right thing.

Addison let go of Gray's hand to clap hers together. "Perfect. The night's going to be amazing."

Gray snagged Addison's hand again and met Jasper's eyes across the desk. "Beyond perfect, babe." Gray's look seemed to communicate his friend harbored additional plans for Addison's book launch.

Oblivious to the silent conversation, Addison stood, pulling Gray up. "Thank you again. We won't take up any more of your time."

"Make sure you pass along your publisher's contact info to Gray. I'll have marketing set up a meeting with you and them to get the ball rolling."

Addison reached across the desk and squeezed Jess's hand. "Your photographs are stunning. Thank you for allowing me to use them." Then she tapped her finger against the back of Jess's ink-covered hand. "If you have any showcasing your beautiful tattoos, I'd love to look at them. Let's grab lunch next time I'm in the city."

"I might have one or two you'd be interested in. I'll go through my prints and bring a selection for you when we do lunch." Jess beamed.

Seconds away from walking out the door, Gray turned with a devious smirk on his lips. "Just the photographs, though. Your abstract art needs a little polishing," he said, nodding toward the window.

"Oh my God, Gray," Addison admonished and yanked him out the door.

Yet they heard him say, "I knew I smelled sex and satisfaction when I walked in." The door closed in his wake, silencing his laughter.

An adorable snort-giggle escaped Jess, making Jasper chuckle. "Ready to head home, sweetheart?"

He heard her yawn, and then she nodded her head against his chest. "Yes."

Jasper tried not to jostle her while he opened a desk drawer. He pulled out a pair of soft ballet flats in her size and slipped them onto her feet. Then he lifted her off his lap to stand between his legs and removed her leash.

"Playtime's over, sweet girl." He tucked it into his jacket pocket, then draped it around Jess, loving how delicate she looked. "I promise I'll fuck you to sleep when we get home."

She brought the collar of his jacket to her nose, breathing him in. "Okay."

Damn. Jasper hoped Sam didn't mind breaking the speed limit.

"I texted Sam, and he's meeting us at the staff entrance. We can take the back stairs and avoid the crowd." He tucked Jess into his side, exiting the club without running into anyone else, and found Sam waiting by the car, holding the door open.

CHAPTER TWENTY-THREE

Jasper

"Jones?" When the nurse called their name, her gaze shifted around the waiting room, going past them, then circling back when Jasper tipped his head.

The appointment for their tests with the fertility specialist arrived.

The deep breath Jess expelled beside him revealed her nerves. Jasper laced their fingers together and lifted her hand to his lips. "You and me together, sweetheart. All the way. We're the Jones'," he said, stating the obvious when he helped Jess to her feet.

They followed the nurse down the hall with doors numbered one through four. She stopped them at door number three and handed Jasper another plastic container.

"We need a sperm sample," the nurse said, flipping through their chart. "The room contains options to assist you if needed."

"I'd prefer my wife's assistance."

The nurse looked between them, a smile quirking her lips. "We don't care how it gets in the cup. Just make sure it gets in the cup. Questions?"

"No. We're good," Jasper answered, ignoring Jessica's gasp and her subtle attempt to let go of his hand. Jasper tightened his grip, settling her indignation.

The nurse gave him the tiniest smile, then schooled her features before unlocking the door. She gestured for them to enter. "Take all the time you need." Then she left them, and Jasper locked the door.

"Jasper Jones," Jess whisper-shouted; spinning to face him, she yanked her hand free. "That's not funny." She glared at him with her fists clenched. Fuck, he loved it when she got all feisty.

"It's a little bit funny. And besides," Jasper said, waving a hand toward the beige walls and the unassuming couch and chair making up the room. "You're providing the one thing guaranteed to get them their sample. You."

"Do not seduce me with your sweet words in the middle of a doctor's clinic."

"Is it working?"

"Yes. I mean, no. Damn it, Jasper. Everyone's going to know what we're doing in here."

"Of course, everyone will know what we're doing in here. It's the same damn thing other folks are most likely doing behind doors one, two, and four."

Jasper tugged Jess into his arms and traced his fingertips along her temple, tucking a wayward strand of hair behind her ear. "I'm sorry I didn't tell you my plan. Today is a lot for both of us, and I figured we might get things done while releasing some tension. Forgive me?" Jasper knew he'd succeeded when Jess wrapped her arms around his neck.

"Fine. It's for the greater good, after all," Jess agreed. Jasper nuzzled the spot beneath her ear to distract her, and Jess tilted her head, giving him more access to lick and nip at her throat. "Mm," she groaned, then pulled away from him.

"Jess?"

She stepped further away until her back pressed against the door. She dragged her hand down her throat, tracing the ghosts of his kisses, then she made a demand of her own, "Take out your cock."

Jasper shook his head, and a growl rumbled deep in his chest. "Jess...this isn't your photography studio, and this isn't how we do things."

"Well, we didn't have a 'medical clinic wank room' negotiated in our contract, either."

Jasper smirked, and his cock thickened. "Touche." He slipped his hands into his pockets, pulling the fabric tighter, making her aware of what she did to him.

"Alright, since we're in uncharted territory, what are your terms?" He knew Jess didn't expect him to throw down negotiation tactics with his dick tenting his pants. He did, however, enjoy keeping his wife on her toes.

"I...um...what if we took turns?"

"Took turns, how?"

"Oh, I don't know...." *Oh, he believed she did.* "I can command you to do something. You command me to do something. So on and so on."

"So on and so on, eh?" Jasper took a step toward her. With nowhere for her to go, Jess held up her hand, stopping him from taking another step.

"No touching each other. We -" Jess licked her lips. "We touch ourselves. After all, the point is to get it all in the cup."

"Indeed." Jasper flicked the lid off the cup under discussion and set it on the table beside him. "What about your mouth?"

"What about it?" His eyes tracked the hand she dragged down her throat, over her breasts, down her stomach, and in between her thighs, rubbing her pussy through the leggings she wore.

"You're playing dirty, Jessica. Now, move your hand away from your delectable pussy and answer my question."

She took her sweet-ass time, sliding those fingers away from her core. The growl grew louder the longer she didn't answer. Jasper took another ominous step closer. "No mouth," she gasped. "Everything goes in the cup."

Jasper's growl reached a crescendo, and it crossed his mind that those behind doors one, two, and four might receive an immersive audio experience besides what was happening in their respective rooms. "Fine. I want to look at all of you. Strip."

"Everything remains on below the waist for me. While you get to leave your shirt on and take off your pants. Last offer."

Jasper stared Jessica down, more turned on than he ever expected to be amid a doctor's clinic. "Fuck, I am going to bend you over every surface in our house when we get home. Your ass will turn red with the help of my palm and any other implement I choose to use."

He took another step closer. "Then I'm going to fuck your mouth, your pussy, and your ass. And you won't come until I give you permission to do so. Do we have a deal?"

"Will you push me to my limits?" she asked, her voice filled with anticipation and desire.

Jasper gave her a wicked smile and said, "Right to the edge."

"Deal."

Jasper reached for a towel, folded it, and set it at his feet. "Get on your knees, sweetheart."

"Take your cock out," she demanded for the second time while lowering into the position, never taking her eyes off him, and he happily complied.

He undid his belt and slid it from the loops. He folded it in half and snapped the leather, which echoed in the clinical room. "This will come in handy when I get you home." The button and zipper on the dark denim he wore followed, and he let his jeans fall below his waist.

"Take off your top," he commanded, biting down on his bottom lip when Jess pulled the material over her head, leaving her in black lace, which did nothing to hide her hard, pierced nipples. "Bra, too." Fuck, he loved her tits. And for a guy who fucking hated needles, he sure loved the fuck out of her piercings.

Jess didn't rush to remove her bra like she did her shirt. She teased him and herself by running her fingers over her lace-covered peaks. Her moan accompanied his own when her fingers dipped beneath the lace and tugged on the rings.

"Jasper, please," she whimpered, her gaze never wavering from the defined line of his erection beneath his black boxer briefs.

Jasper gripped the base of his cock through his underwear. "I'll show you mine if you show me yours," he said with a wicked chuckle.

Jess trailed her fingers along her collarbone, tracing her sexy tattoos. She tugged her bra strap down her arm, doing the same on her other side, and when she reached behind to unhook the clasp, her nipples crested the top of the lace cups.

"Oh fuck, yeah." He reached beneath the waistband and pulled his cock and balls free from his underwear, and her bra dropped to the floor.

"Play with them for me. Tug on your rings," Jasper commanded her.

Jess cupped her breasts, drawing her thumb and index fingers toward her nipples, squeezing them until she held the rings between her fingers. She pulled and twisted them while her hips rocked, searching for some relief.

"Stroke your dick for me," she countered. Back and forth their commands went.

Jasper held his palm beneath her bottom lip. "Spit." Jess obliged, and he slicked his cock in her saliva, stroking himself from root to tip.

"Faster."

"Get your hand in your pants and play with your pretty pussy, then. This won't take much longer. You look fucking perfect on your knees for me. I love you, Jess."

"Love you, too." Her fingers slipped beneath her waistband, and she moaned. "I'm fucking drenched for you."

"I can hear it. Can fucking smell your sweet arousal. Fuck, I'm close." He worked himself faster.

"Hold off for me."

Jasper slowed his hand and squeezed the tip of his dick to stave off his orgasm. His efforts almost didn't matter when Jess leaned forward and kissed his testicles.

Jasper shuddered and, between clenched teeth, said, "Thought you said no mouth."

"I did, didn't I? We can compromise a little." Jess reached over and grabbed the cup off the table, opened her mouth, tipped her head back, and placed the plastic between her teeth.

"Oh, sweet fuck. Are you close, Jess? Looking at you like this, I can't hold back any longer. I need you right there with me," Jasper gasped, giving her one last command.

The cup between her teeth didn't hamper the "Yes" he heard loud and clear.

His balls drew tight to his body, and his orgasm tingled at the base of his spine. Jess moaned when her release crashed over her, and while her body rocked through the spasms, her head and the cup didn't move.

"Oh fuck, Jess. I'm coming," he hissed. The heat of his orgasm traveled the length of his cock, and he stroked himself, landing ropes of hot cum into the container until it almost reached the top.

Jasper took a deep breath and squeezed the last of his cum from his tip. He took the container from Jess's mouth, not letting any of it spill, capped it, and set it on the table with a shaky hand.

"You are fucking beautiful, Jess."

Jasper cupped her face in his hands and kissed her, deepening it when she parted her lips. He traced his tongue along her bottom lip, slipping inside her mouth to tangle with hers.

"Love you, sweetheart," he whispered against her lips when they parted.

"Love you, too." Jess pressed against his thigh, hugging his leg.

"Up you go." He offered her his hand and helped her to her feet. They straightened their clothes and washed up in the nearby sink, giggling like teenagers, knowing the warm glow on their cheeks and satisfied smiles showed how successful they were.

"Holy shit," Jess exclaimed, picking up the container. "Should we dump some out? It seems excessive for a sample."

"No way," Jasper said, snatching it from her hand. "We worked hard to provide every one of these swimmers. We're not dumping any of them down the drain."

Jess burst out laughing and doubled over in a fit of giggles. "Oh, my god. The look on your face." She snorted, making him chuckle.

"Alright, come on. Let's hand these bad boys over, and if they need nothing else, we can get out of here and grab some lunch."

Jess took a deep breath and shook her limbs, stemming the rest of her giggles. She nestled her hand in the crook of his elbow and leaned her head against his shoulder. "Sounds good. I'm starving. Getting you off worked up quite the appetite."

"I bet." He deadpanned, which sent Jess into another round of giggles.

When she got things under control, Jess hesitated by the door with a blush staining her cheeks. Jasper stepped in front of her, disengaging the lock and peeking into the hall. "Coast's clear," he said, and Jess took his hand when they stepped out of the room.

Across the hall, a sign telling them 'samples go here' hung above a tray built into the counter, frosted plexiglass divided it from staff on the other side where Jasper placed his cup. Seconds later, he swore he heard a drawn-out "Damn" from the other side of the wall.

Jess snorted and smacked his chest, giving him a look that screamed, 'I told you'

They pulled it together by the time the nurse came around the corner. She stopped beside the counter, and a gloved hand from the other side of the plexiglass took his sample away.

Jess disguised her little snort-giggle with a cough when the nurse's brows approached her hairline. It took everything in Jasper not to laugh, too.

"Mr. and Mrs. Jones, since you've submitted your sample, we need nothing further from you today. We'll call in a week when the test results are ready and have you come in then. Dr. Cline will review everything with you and discuss your options." The nurse gave them a smile, then turned and headed back to where she came.

Jasper pulled Jess to his side and kissed her temple. "Now, all we need to do is wait. Lucky for you, I have plans to make the wait worthwhile," he growled. Jess shivered with anticipation, and it was all the confirmation he needed.

Chapter Twenty-Four

Jess

*J*ess gasped when her nipples touched the cold granite counter. Jasper's grip on the back of her neck held her in place in the middle of their kitchen, and the sudden chill heightened her arousal. She whimpered when he struck her ass.

"More," she begged.

Jasper grunted next to her ear with the force of his next smack. "Naughty girl. Did you believe I'd let your wicked cock-hardening negotiations earlier go unpunished?"

"Never. I want it. Need it," Jess cried, writhing beneath him.

She shuddered when Jasper growled, "What do you need, pet?"

The words tumbled from her lips. "For you to make it hurt."

"Mm...the answer I hoped for." From the corner of her eye, she watched Jasper reach for the wooden spoon amongst the cooking utensils they kept in a canister on the counter....

Jess shifted in her seat, relishing the pleasurable ache remaining from Jasper fucking every one of her holes after he finished reddening her ass and thighs with his palm and a wooden spoon.

Unfortunately, this morning brought reality crashing around them.

"Everything alright, sweetheart? The blush highlighting your cheeks tells me what's occupying your mind." Then he said in a low voice next to her ear. "I can't get last night out of my mind, either."

Jess met his gaze. "Better than the alternative, isn't it?"

"If wicked memories keep you grounded, who am I to deny you?" Jasper raised their entwined hands and kissed her knuckles, easing the tension in her grip.

She gave him a smile for his efforts. It didn't detract from receiving a call to come back to Dr. Cline's office not even twenty-four hours after getting their tests done.

Despite being alone, Jess dropped her voice to a whisper. "And no, everything's not alright, and you know it. Something bad showed up on one of our tests." Jess didn't want to cry, but her eyes burned with unshed tears.

Jasper turned in his seat and pressed her hand against his chest; holding her gaze, he looked deep into her eyes and said, "If there is, we face it together."

"How are you this calm?" She sniffled, and Jasper plucked a tissue from the box on the edge of the desk, handing it to her.

"I'm not."

"But-?" Jess searched his eyes for answers he didn't have.

Jasper leaned in close, and his breath ghosted over her lips like a tender caress. "No buts. I'm scared, but I'll be strong enough for the both of us."

"Didn't you say 'no buts?'" she teased, trying to shake the cloud of doom and gloom from the room. Then the office door opened, silencing their chatter, and dread again hung over them.

This is it.

This is when the other shoe drops. Jess took a fortifying breath, and she and Jasper shifted back into their seats when the petite, dark-haired doctor entered the room and sat in the chair behind the desk.

Dr. Cline clasped her hands above the file she brought and gave them an assessing look. "Thank you for coming, and I apologize for the rush. This is something you needed to know right away."

Jess tightened her grip on Jasper's hand, bracing herself for the bad news. Jasper readied to take the blow for her and asked, "What is it?"

"Well." Dr. Cline leaned forward, and Jess held her breath when a bright smile transformed the doctor's face. "You don't require my expertise. Congratulations. You're pregnant."

Pregnant?

Neither she nor Jasper said a fucking word, and Dr. Cline filled them in while oblivious to the fact she'd rocked their world off its axis.

"From the date you gave us for your last period, we calculate you to be about six weeks along. However, we can confirm this with a transvaginal ultrasound. It's too soon for the fetus to register on a pelvic scan."

Wait...how's this possible?

Jess didn't ask the sensible question. Instead, she did some quick math and blurted, "Oh my god. The night in the dungeon."

Dr. Cline's eyes widened. "Pardon? Did you say dungeon?"

"Sorry, I'm in shock. Did you say I'm pregnant?"

"Yes."

"How's this possible? I mean, I know how. How is this possible for me? I can't get pregnant." The hand not gripped in Jasper's shook when she slid it over her lower abdomen and stared down at her flat stomach with utter disbelief.

Is this real?

Dr. Cline's expression softened. "I reviewed your file and compared it with the tests we did here. Your original results were correct; you had a less than three percent chance of conceiving, but that's still a chance." Dr. Cline gave them an assessing look. "You both admitted to being apart for an extended period where neither one of you took part in sexual activity, correct?"

Jess glanced at Jasper, but his gaze remained fixated on Dr. Cline. "Um, yes, that's correct."

The doctor leaned back in her chair and said, "Sometimes there isn't any other explanation except the two of you connected in the right place at the right time." Dr. Cline's lips quirked with a hint of a smile. "Your husband's sperm is also quite...um...potent."

Dr. Cline flipped through the pages of their file. "We ran the urine and blood tests four times to be sure."

Jess wasn't sure how to wrap her head around such unexpected news. "Can you believe it, Jas? I never thought this would be possible. We're having a baby."

Jess turned in her chair, expecting the same unexpected excitement and wonder from Jasper. Instead, she found him pale with sweat glistening on his forehead. "Jasper?"

The grip Jasper had on her hand tightened to an almost painful level.

"Is everything alright?" Dr. Cline asked.

"Dr. Cline, can you please give us a moment?" Jess asked, not taking her eyes off her husband.

"Yes, of course," she said, getting up. Jess heard something open and close behind her, and a cold bottle of water appeared near her elbow. "It will help. Take all the time you need. I'll be in the room adjoining this office. When you're ready, I'll do your ultrasound." She kept her tone low and soothing, which Jess appreciated.

"Thank you."

Jess didn't wait a second longer beyond the door closing and crawled into Jasper's lap. She clasped his face between the palms of her hands. "Hey…I'm here, Jas. I want you to focus on my voice and breathe with me. Okay?"

Jasper gave her a sharp nod.

"Good, my love. You need to slow those breaths down for me." She dragged her fingers through his hair and gripped the back of his neck, pressing her forehead to his. "In through your nose and out through your mouth." She kept her voice soft, doing the breathing with him.

She picked up Jasper's trembling hand and placed it against her sternum. "Follow the rise and fall of my chest. I'm here, Jasper. I'm not going anywhere."

Jasper fought to relax his tense muscles, and his words came out fast between his clenched teeth. "Sorry…fucked you hard last night. Did I…hurt you or the baby?" His gaze darted toward her stomach, and he tried to shift away. Jess tightened her grip on his neck, keeping him still and focused on her.

"I'm fine. I promise. You didn't hurt me or the baby."

"Jess."

"Shh, I swear. Keep your breathing steady, love. Don't try to talk yet. We can address any concerns with the doctor. Then you and I will discuss what works best for us while this pregnancy progresses. It will be okay."

Jess wasn't just trying to convince Jasper; she was doing her damndest to convince herself of it, too.

"Okay," Jasper said, sounding wary. "Yeah...we'll be talking about this. A lot." He closed his eyes, and the corner of his mouth quirked with the hint of a grin.

There's her sweet, dominant husband.

Jasper calmed, and when his eyes fluttered open, Jess grabbed the water and opened it. "Here, drink this," she whispered, holding the bottle to his lips. He drained half of it in seconds.

"Fuck. That hasn't happened to me since my folks died. A fucking panic attack. We got the most incredible news, and my mind spiraled, replacing the memories of what Joanna went through with you. I couldn't stop it."

Jess's heart ached for her husband. He survived harrowing military missions, the death of his parents, raising his teenage sister, launching the club, Jess leaving him without a word for three years, and he still accepted her back with open arms.

"Jasper, you are the strongest person I know. What Jo and Jon went through won't happen to us."

"How do you know?"

She held his face between her palms and looked deep into his eyes. "I know because you and I aren't them. Their experience isn't ours, and we'll take our journey one day at a time."

Jasper exhaled a shuddering breath. "You're right. I love you. I love you so much, sweetheart," he said, his voice thick with emotion.

Jess caressed his bottom lip with her thumb and kissed him with the reverence he deserved. "I love you, too. This moment has shown me how we are each other's strengths. I will be here for you. The way I should've been. The way you are for me."

"Fuck, I love you so fucking much, Jess. A lifetime will never be enough time with you."

"Ready to get our first look at this little person in the making?"

Jasper's hand scorched a path from her sternum to her stomach, where he covered her belly. Jess tried and failed to hold back tears when he asked, "This is real? We're having a baby?"

Jess covered Jasper's hand with hers. "So the good doctor says. However, I'm having a hard time believing it's real. This wasn't supposed to be possible."

She looked toward the closed door, hoping Dr. Cline was still waiting. "Don't know about you, Jas, but I need some tangible proof. The validation of our little embryo on the screen and hearing the strong beat of its heart. I won't believe it's real until we do."

Jasper cupped her face, catching the tears trailing down her cheeks. "I love you," he whispered, then kissed her lips again. "Let's go meet our kid."

"Alright, there'll be a bit of pressure."

Easy for the Doc to say when she didn't have an ultrasound wand pushing against her cervix. Jess did her best to ignore it and kept her eyes glued to the screen.

Jasper kissed her forehead and whispered, "You're doing great, sweetheart."

"So are you," she whispered back.

"Here we are." Dr. Cline pointed at the screen, and Jess's breath froze in her chest, and her eyes filled with tears again. "This is the amniotic sac and the bean-shaped group of cells in the middle is your baby." Dr. Cline pressed another button, and the whirring thump of their baby's heartbeat filled the room.

Jess sobbed, and tears cascaded down her cheeks. "It's real? I'm pregnant?" She looked up to find Jasper in a similar state with the biggest grin on his face.

Jasper pulled out his phone and hit record, capturing the vibrant sound of their baby's heartbeat.

"Congratulations. Based on these measurements, the date of your conception is correct. If all goes well, you'll hold your baby in your arms eight months from now." Dr. Cline captured the image on the screen and removed the wand. "I'll print you a copy."

"Please," they both said.

"Meet me in my office once you've dressed, and I'll answer your questions."

"Thank you."

The moment the door clicked shut, Jasper pulled Jess into a sitting position and wrapped her in his arms. He buried his face in her neck, breathing her in, making her shiver. "Holy fuck, sweetheart. We're having a baby," he said against her throat.

Jess stared at the frozen image on the screen. "I'm scared, Jasper."

"Me too. Terrified may be a better way to describe it. Let's try to focus on how many things can go right." He kissed her. The salty taste of his tears mingled with hers when Jasper's tongue slipped past her lips when he deepened the kiss.

"Come on," he said, helping her stand. Jess didn't realize how much her hands trembled until she tried to pull her pants up herself, and Jasper needed to help her.

"I want to take you home, cuddle on the couch, stare at the picture, and listen to the recording of their heartbeat. Our tiny miracle. I need to know you're safe, and I won't breathe easily until I'm holding you in my arms."

Jess cupped Jasper's face and tangled her fingers in his beard to pull him close. She kissed his lips and said, "Please, Jas. I need that, too."

CHAPTER TWENTY-FIVE

Jasper

J ess was almost three months pregnant, sporting the most adorable baby bump Jasper had ever seen, and tonight, Joanna and Jonathan were the first people they planned to tell.

Jasper expelled a deep breath and opened the door for Joanna, who held a wiggling Sara-Jane while Jon grabbed everything from the car.

"Hey," Joanna exclaimed, and Jasper bent, offering his cheek for her incoming kiss and his arms to collect his wiggling niece. He snuggled her into the crook of his elbow in time for his sister's inquisition.

"Long time no see, brother mine. I almost forgot what you look like." Her hands moved to her hips while she leveled him with her most practiced glare. "Care to explain why you and Jess have avoided me beyond texts and calls for the past month?"

Sara-Jane lifted her tiny fingers into Jasper's beard and tugged with surprising strength while a toothless grin lit her face.

Jasper ignored his sister's interrogation in favor of the little girl in his arms. "Ah, sweet Janie, your mom will have her answers soon enough."

"What do you mean? Has something changed? Did you sell the club? Are you moving? What are you keeping from your favorite sister?"

"Jeez, Jo...the way your mind works. Also, none of those are even close."

"My mind is beautiful, and I've plenty more ideas where those came from."

Jasper groaned and said, "It's what I'm afraid of." His voice softened when he returned his attention to Sara-Jane. "Let's find Auntie Jess and say hello. Can't have your mom coming up with any other worst-case scenarios."

"Those aren't my worst-case scenarios," Joanna mumbled.

"You don't need to share those either," Jasper countered. "It's good news, sister mine. I promise."

With his arms laden with bags, Jonathan pushed the door closed with his elbow and grumbled, "Didn't even get to say hello, and he's already strolled off with our kid. We talked about this babe, bro time, then he gets niece time."

Jasper smirked when he poked his head around the corner. " Get your butt in the house faster next time." Sara-Jane joined his laughter with a hearty squeal, making Jess look up when he entered the dining room.

Her gaze traveled over him and his niece, and the look she gave him smoldered. *Interesting.* Jess bit down on her bottom lip and closed the distance between them.

"Do you know how effing hot you look in uncle-daddy mode?" Jess whispered in his ear.

"Effing?"

"I'm trying to work on my swearing habits."

Jasper chuckled. "Good luck with that. Any children raised around us will know the many nuances of the word fuck by age three. No matter how hard we try to use alternatives."

Jess sighed, which made him laugh more. "I suppose you're right, which means the PTA parents will hate us."

"Screw the PTA."

Jess's laughter morphed into a cough when Joanna asked, "What's all this beef with the PTA?"

"Joanna," Jess exclaimed, popping around him to wrap his sister in a warm embrace. "I've missed you."

"Missed you, too." She said, pulling back to look at Jessica with a critical eye. "Now, why are parents and teachers going to hate you?"

Jonathan's arrival gave Jess the excuse not to answer. "Hi, Jon."

"Hey Jess," he said, kissing her cheek. "I'm going to help myself to a beer while you clue my wife in on the fact you and Jasper are adding to your family. Congrats, by the way."

Well, there's one way to break the news.

"What?" Joanna moved back, not letting go of Jess's arms, and dragged her calculating gaze over her, putting the pieces together. "Wait...you're glowing. And your boobs look fantastic. I wanted to know what bra you were wearing." Joanna looked into Jess's eyes. "The fantasticness of your boobs isn't because of a bra, is it?"

"No, Jo," Jess said, her laughter shifting to tears.

"Hey," Jasper said, keeping his voice low. He wrapped his free arm around his wife. "Why don't we sit? We can enjoy dinner and tell you everything." Jasper helped Jess into her chair, then placed Sara-Jane in the highchair they got for her visits.

Jon set their drinks on the table and held out Joanna's chair. When he whispered something in her ear, Joanna's expression filled with such love that Jasper thanked his lucky stars again for introducing Jonathan to his sister.

Once they sat down, everyone stared at one another, and no one said a word until Jess cleared her throat. "I never got to tell you why I walked away three years ago." Jasper squeezed her hand, encouraging her to go on.

"I didn't let anyone know I went for some tests. Fertility tests. My doctor at the time told me I'd never get pregnant, and it broke me. In my devastation, I removed myself from Jasper's life, from all your lives."

"Oh, Jessica, no."

Jess gave her a sad smile. "It's okay, Jo, I swear. When I came to my senses, I believed too much time had passed to repair the damage I caused, but when Jasper and I found each other the way, we did." Jess glanced at him, and he gave her an encouraging smile. "It fixed the trajectory of our lives."

Jess stared at their niece, then turned her gaze on Joanna and Jon. "Sara-Jane healed you in tremendous ways. She's also the catalyst for Jasper and me being here today. She has changed all our lives for the better and doesn't even know it."

Jasper did his best to swallow around the emotions clogging his throat. His wife was right. Without Sara-Jane...well, he didn't even want to consider the possibility of not finding Jessica when he did. "Someday, she'll know because we get to tell her." He kissed Jess's hand and whispered, "Love you."

"Love you, too."

Jess reached across the table with her free hand, and Joanna met her halfway. "I wanted to tell you after you shared what you went through, but I needed to tell Jasper first."

"I know you did. It's why I stopped you from saying anything."

"Thank you, but you deserved an explanation. I'm sorry, Jo. You're my best friend, and I didn't allow you to be there for me either."

"Nope. No way. We talked about this. No more apologizing, Jess. We're good. Now, please confirm the reason for the Hollywood glow and big boobs."

Jess snorted. "They're not big."

"Got a strong suspicion they're going to get bigger," Joanna retorted with a devious snort.

"You're right," Jasper interjected, picking up the conversation when their laughter died.

For a second, panic threatened the edge of his consciousness, and he fought back, using the tools his therapist gave him. Jess's steady grip on his hand helped even more.

Jasper released a steadying breath and said, "Joanna, if anything I'm about to say is too much for you, tell me to stop. Goes for you too, Jon."

"Jasper, I promise you, Jonathan and I are good. Sara-Jane has healed those wounds. And while I'm not trying to steal your thunder, big brother, we have news, too. We applied to become foster parents."

"Oh wow. I know it's something you've always wanted to do. You'll be amazing foster parents because you already are amazing parents," Jess said, squeezing Joanna's hand.

"You two have an abundance of love and care to give. I know any child who needs it will find a safe and loving home with you."

"Thank you," Joanna said with pride. "Now spill."

"Okay, okay. Last month, Jess and I got a second opinion from a different specialist to get a better picture of what our options would be. They called us to come in the next day when we didn't expect any news for at least a week."

"And?" His sister asked with anticipation.

"And...while we feared the worst, Jess and I received the most amazing and unexpected news."

"Will you stop torturing us? You're having a baby, aren't you?"

"Yes, we're pregnant," Jess finished, leaning in to wipe a tear from his cheek, and she whispered, "I love you, Jas."

Joanna squealed and jumped from her seat; rounding the table, she wrapped him and Jess in her arms. Or a more accurate description is strangling their necks with utter enthusiasm.

"OhmygodOhmygodOhmygod!" she chanted next to their ears. Then, like Jasper feared, her excitement shifted into a broken sob. "Are you sure? What if...?" Joanna didn't finish the question, unable to speak her fear aloud.

Jasper turned and wrapped his arms around his sister. "No, what ifs. We're taking this day-by-day, sister mine. And each day is better than the last. Are you okay, Jo?"

Joanna loosened her grip and met his gaze. "I am over the moon with happiness for you both. This baby is your miracle like Sara-Jane is ours."

Not for the first time, Jasper wished his parents still lived and were a part of days like today.

Exhausted, Jasper rubbed a hand over his face after showing Joanna and Jonathan to the door with a sleeping Sara-Jane in their arms. He headed upstairs to their bedroom, ready to fuck his wife into dreamland when he heard Jess let out an anguished cry.

Oh, no. Oh, fuck. No.

"Jessica," he shouted.

Jasper raced up the rest of the stairs, where he found Jess lying across the middle of their bed with tears streaming down her cheeks, holding her shirt away from her body.

His heart plummeted, and he pulled out his phone to call 9-1-1. "What's wrong? Is it the baby?" he asked, rushing to her side.

"Oh god, sorry, no. Nothing's wrong with the baby. I didn't mean to scare you." He palmed her swollen belly, and Jess covered his hand with hers. "The baby's okay, I swear. It's my...," her words trailed off on a groan.

Jasper looked at the way Jess alternated between clasping her breasts and holding the material of her top away from her chest. "I don't understand. Are you hurt?"

"My nipples are on fire."

"What?" Shocked by her answer, Jasper searched her chest for actual flames.

Jess groaned and rubbed her tear-stained cheeks. "Not literally."

"Oh, um, okay. Right. What can I do to help?" Jasper asked, setting his phone on the nightstand to keep it nearby.

Jess gave him the saddest look, her lower lip jutting into a pout. "You're going to have to remove my nipple rings. I don't want to take them out. I have to," she said with a sob.

Jasper knew this day was coming. Jess wanted to try breastfeeding, and they'd need to be removed at some point. He wouldn't have minded a little more time. It sounded like Jess felt the same way.

Jess lifted her top over her head, baring her fuller breasts. Her nipples had darkened, and the weight of her piercings tugged the swollen tips. Even the veins crisscrossing her chest appeared more vibrant and visible beneath her skin.

"Fuck, you're beautiful, Jessica." Jasper wanted to trace those veins with his lips, following a path toward her sensitive nipples.

"Ugh, hormones. Welcome to the stage of pregnancy where flames are licking my tits, and I'm crazy horny."

Jess rocked her hips, and the cool air in the room hardened her nipples to tight little buds, making her whimper, groan, and writhe all at once. His dick hardened within the confines of his pants, on board with his plan to turn her pain into pleasure.

Jasper leaned close, pressing kisses along her jaw and down her neck. "I believe there's a way I can help."

Jess tilted her head, giving him more access. "I'm listening."

"It's better if I show you." Jasper grabbed hold of his collar and pulled his shirt over his head, then he slid his palms over her ribs until his thumbs and index fingers framed the bottom of her luscious, swollen tits.

"This okay?" he asked. Jess nodded. "And how about this?" Jasper bent his head and swirled his tongue around the ring, piercing her left nipple.

"Oh, that feels good."

He pulled back, admiring her swollen flesh glistening with his saliva. Then he leaned over and captured the other between his lips, lavishing it with the same attention.

Jess whimpered and rocked her hips, searching for him. Jasper kept his cock out of her reach, wanting to take his time with her.

"Patience, sweetheart. Let me take care of you."

Jasper reached for the lotion Jess kept on her nightstand and squirted some into his hands, massaging the cool liquid into her skin. Jess bit her lip and groaned, arching into his touch, wanting more. "How's the pressure? Is it too little or too much?"

"Mm...no. It's just right."

Jasper chuckled. "This isn't Goldie Locks and the Three Bears, little girl."

"Less teasing and more rubbing of the boobs."

"Whatever you need, sweetheart." Jasper trailed kisses over her swollen belly. When his lips reached her covered mound, he whispered, "Take off your pants."

Jess wiggled her hips, sliding the material down her body until he could nuzzle the soft skin at the juncture of her thigh.

He breathed her in and groaned, "Fuck, I want to bathe in your scent, sweetheart. Spread your legs for me."

Jessica shifted beneath him, widening her legs to accommodate him when he settled between her thighs. Jasper kept his hands on her breasts and balanced on his elbows, caging her in by her hips. He admired her glistening pussy. "You're fucking soaked for me, Jess. Fuck, I need to taste you."

"Please, Jas."

"Love the way you beg me. Never stop."

"Please...I need your mouth on me. Your tongue fucking me and making me come."

Jasper dragged his nose along the crease of her thigh, taking her sweet, musky scent deep into his lungs. "Yes, sweetheart. Gonna make you come until you're limp and satisfied." He pressed his tongue between her folds, parting her pussy lips in search of her clit.

"Yes...please, I need it."

Jasper groaned the moment his mouth filled with the taste of her sweet ambrosia. "Fuck, peaches." He circled her clit with his tongue, sucking her swollen bud between his lips. "Grab the lotion, Jess, and keep massaging those gorgeous tits. You need my magic fingers elsewhere."

Jess laughed. "Damn, you walk a fine line between corny and sexy." She squealed when he slapped four fingers against her splayed open cunt.

"You're distracting me from my goal of making you come. Now, let me give you what you need." Jasper went back to sucking her clit, her cunt spread open, ready and waiting for him to worship. Jess clenched around the two fingers he slid inside her when he flicked her swollen bud with his tongue.

Jess locked her legs around him and arched her back, letting out a long, drawn-out moan while he worked the pads of his fingers against her g-spot. "Jasper, I'm close. Please don't stop."

"Yes, sweetheart. Don't hold back. Come for me." Jasper added another finger, filling her tight cunt and fucking her faster.

Doubling his efforts, Jasper sucked and flicked her clit when the first flutters of her orgasm hit. The way her pussy clenched around his fingers made his cock weep with envy. Jessica's pleasure was his pleasure.

She flooded his hand with her release and cried out his name, riding the waves of her orgasm. He slowed his strokes, bringing her back down to earth after she shattered for him. Jasper sucked her labia, licking into her opening, seeking her cream, giving her sensitized clit a break.

Jess whimpered his name, and Jasper's balls tightened. His orgasm tingled at the base of his spine. "Fuck. Every little noise you make drives me wild.

Everything about you…it will never be enough. I swear, Jess. I won't waver. This time, I'll follow you into the dark."

"Jasper." She used the grip on his hair to pull him up her body, her lips finding his, tasting herself on his tongue while she explored his mouth. "I love you," she whispered against his lips.

Not even close to being finished, Jasper kissed his way back down her body. Nestled between her legs and held her gaze while he teased her clit with the tip of his tongue. He circled her needy bud, ramping Jess toward another release.

"Everything, Jess. I want it all…."

When Jessica's shaky legs fell from his shoulders after her fourth orgasm, Jasper knew she reached her limit. He sat up and wiped his mouth with the back of his hand.

Jess reached for him when he tried to stand. "Jasper, wait." He froze, crouched over her, and met her hooded gaze. "What about you?" she asked.

He gave her a rueful chuckle and said, "Came in my pants the moment I wrenched a third orgasm out of you." He bent over and gave her a gentle kiss. "Give me a second to clean up, then I'll take care of you."

Once he'd cleaned the remnants of multiple orgasms from her sated body, Jasper opened the drawer in Jess's nightstand, removing a slim gold chain with a tiny key hanging from it.

Jasper cupped her right breast and kissed her nipple, then he inserted the key into the tiny hole and removed the ring, doing the same on her other side.

He held the warm metal in his hand and caught the solitary tear, slipping down Jess's cheek with his thumb.

"It's okay, sweetheart, it's not forever."

"I know." She sniffled.

"This doesn't change our bond, contract, or commitment to one another." He unclasped the chain, dropped her rings onto it, and draped it around his neck. "Let me carry these for you until you can wear them again."

"Okay." While her tears flowed unchecked, the smile she gave him radiated happiness. Jess pulled him close for another kiss. "Thank you for knowing what I needed. I love you, Jasper."

CHAPTER TWENTY-SIX

Jasper

"Yesss. I got my signed copy," Jess exclaimed, tucking it against her chest. "I can't wait to read it."

"Isn't it the same book Addie gave you an advanced copy of? You've already read it."

"I haven't read the signed version yet," she said, giving Jasper an adorable pout.

"Right." Jasper knew which part she looked forward to rereading most, and it's one he'd love to help her reenact. He pulled Jess close, tucking her into his side. His left hand caressed her rounded belly, and he directed her attention toward the stage, having gotten a heads-up on the festivities.

Jess gasped when she clued in and whispered, "This is when Gray planned to propose to Addie?"

"Yup. Wait. How did you know?"

"He told me the day I met her," she smirked. "Aw...I'm happy for them. I think they're perfect for one another."

"Yes, they are."

Jess and he cheered and applauded along with everyone else when Gray slipped the engagement ring onto Addie's finger.

The lights pulsed, warning the crowd something else was about to unfold, and those not sticking around headed upstairs toward the lobby. Jess straightened in his arms. "Is Gray about to?"

"Why do you think he wore his tearaway leathers? He's presenting the collar he made for Addie. It's more than an engagement. It's also a claiming ceremony." He didn't miss Jess's gaze dropping to the pants in question or the blush warming her cheeks.

"If you want to skip it, we can begin our more private celebrations upstairs. I, for one, have already seen Gray's dick more times than I can count over the years."

She faced him, taking her eyes off the stage. "Oh, uh, you know what? I, too, have seen Gray's dick way more than I expected to in this lifetime. I'm good."

Jasper laughed against her lips, then sealed their mouths in a searing kiss.

"Do you want to get married?" he asked, pulling her into the corner and creating a bubble of privacy for them. Jess stared at him with wide eyes and a speechlessness he didn't expect.

"You got a weird way of proposing something we already are, buddy."

"Buddy?" Jasper growled, knowing Jess said it to provoke him. "I know what we are. Wife." He tugged on the leash, bringing her closer to him. The same one he used to attach to the chain between her breasts, now hooked to a thin leather collar at the base of her throat.

"And I meant a vow renewal to reaffirm our bond." His hand moved from her hip to her belly where a kick connected with his palm. "Huh, even Baby A agrees."

"Sorry, I believe that's Baby B trying to get your attention." Jasper stared in amazement while her stomach rippled beneath her white peasant blouse.

Yup. Jessica's pregnant with twins.

He and Jess found out more than the sex of the baby at their six-teen-week ultrasound. Two baby girls will grace them with their pres-ence in a little over two months. Jasper always saw himself as a girl dad and loved the idea of raising two fierce and independent daughters.

"Yes, I want to marry you. Again." Jess bit down on her bottom lip, silencing the rest of what she wanted to say.

"But?"

"It's not an objection, it's a...not yet."

"What do you mean? I'd love to marry you again on our anniversary; our eighth is four months away."

"I know it is, and I love wanting to renew our vows on our anniversary." Jess sighed and played with the collar of his shirt, not meeting his gaze.

"I want to focus on getting through this pregnancy, Jasper, and not stress over planning a wedding right after they're born. Besides, when I've imagined this and dear husband, I've imagined this. I picture our daughters being part of the celebration."

"You make a sound argument, Wife." Jasper leaned in and kissed her. His tongue teased her soft lips open until she moaned into his mouth. When they broke apart, he pressed his forehead to hers and asked, "What do you propose we do?"

"How about on our tenth? The twins will be a year and a half by then. They might even toddle down the aisle." She got a far-off look on her face, imagining their unborn children doing what she described.

"I can picture it, too, and it sounds perfect. I have one condition," Jasper said, pulling back enough to stare into her eyes.

"Oh? And what's that?"

"If I have to wait two years for us to renew our vows, I want you to marry me every anniversary after that."

"Hmm." Jess tapped her lips, letting the ambient light reflect off the diamond ring he'd given her almost a decade ago. "You also make a sound argument. I agree with your terms."

Jasper kissed the spot below her ear. "I love you, and I love getting what I want."

Jess arched into his touch. "Oh? Well, I want you to take me to the dungeon for a little fun and celebration of our own."

Jasper gripped her jaw and brought her close enough to align their noses, and his lips grazed hers with each word he spoke. "I'm going to tie you down and suck on your sweet tits until you give me a taste of the sustenance you'll provide our children."

Jess's eyes darkened with desire, and Jasper tugged her toward the stairs leading to the private rooms.

At the bottom of those steps, they came face-to-face with Weston Sharpe.

"West? I didn't know you'd be here." Jess's surprise mirrored his own. Though Jasper hoped he'd come back, several months had passed since West helped him rescue his niece.

"I got here in time to catch the proposal and the show," West said, tipping his head toward the stage where the *show* was winding down between the newly engaged and satisfied couple.

Jess jumped into action, wrapping West in a warm embrace. "Welcome home."

"What're yea welcoming me back with, Jess?" he asked when he pulled back, and his gaze dipped to her stomach.

"Babies," Jasper said behind her. "Jess is welcoming you with our babies."

"Babies? More than one?"

"Our twin girls are due in September."

"Lass, you're having wee lasses? You told me...I mean it's fuckin' amazing...but you said..." West's words trailed off, not knowing how to finish that sentence.

"There's a lot to tell you. Shocked doesn't describe finding out we got pregnant. Now, we have to get used to the fact there are two. Lucky for me, they like to give a good swift kick to my bladder and ribs at the same time. It's a helpful reminder."

"The doc said I have potent sperm," Jasper added with a laugh, though it turned into a grunt when Jess elbowed him in the ribs.

"You know that's not quite what the doctor said."

"I heard nothing past her telling us you're pregnant until the whoosh of their heartbeat filled the room." Jasper stared into his wife's eyes, and for a moment, everyone else disappeared.

"For crying out loud, you two are gonna have me shedding sentimental tears in the middle of a sex club. Congratulations, you two, I fuckin mean it." West pulled them both in for another hug.

Jasper didn't miss how his gaze drifted up the stairs for the third time. "Looking for someone?"

"What? No." Yet Jasper caught West's gaze moving to the balcony above them again.

"The club looks great," West said, trying to divert the subject from his wandering eyes. Jasper caught the moment when West landed on what, or more like, who he sought.

Kari.

Jasper chuckled to himself and pulled his keys from his pocket. He took the one for their basement apartment off the ring and handed it to their unexpected guest. "You remember where the brownstone is?"

"Aye."

"The basement apartment is yours until the twins arrive. You've got the next couple of months to figure out if you're making this permanent." Jasper tipped his head toward where Kari stood. "If you haven't already done it, I'll introduce you."

"What're you talking about?" West asked. Since his eyes didn't stray from Kari, there's no denying who Jasper meant.

"She's the one I wanted you to meet." West dragged his gaze from Kari to him. They stared at one another until West looked back at Kari with a slight tip of his chin, acknowledging it, though not quite ready to talk about it.

Jasper hoped he'd be by the following Sunday cause there'd be no avoiding meeting Kari then. "Alright, I'll let it go. For now. Joanna and Jon will expect you at brunch this Sunday when I tell them you're back."

"You know I'll never pass up a home-cooked meal and good company. Count me in." West ran a hand through his hair and used his other hand to cover his yawn. "The jetlag is hitting me pretty hard. Thanks for the place to stay. I'm gonna make use of it."

He turned toward the lobby when Jasper called his name. "West?"

"Yeah?"

"It's good to have you back."

"Thanks, brother. I'll catch you guys later, and congratulations again. You deserve this kind of happiness."

Jess pulled West in for one more hug and said loud enough for Jasper to hear, "You deserve happiness, too." West smiled, then vanished into the crowd. When Jasper glanced back to where Kari stood, she disappeared, too.

"Jasper Jones. Those are some big league matchmaking aspirations you have there."

"Why? You disagree?"

"No, they'd be great together. West will do his best to resist, though."

"At first. But West will understand soon enough. Resistance is futile."

Jess snorted. "Okay, dark lord. Brunch will be interesting this week." His wife glowed with happiness, staring up at him. Her pupils darkened with desire when he tugged on her leash, bringing her against him.

"Indeed," Jasper growled beside her ear while he surrounded her with his body, creating a protective layer between Jess and everyone else. He guided her up the stairs and whispered, "Come, wife. A lifetime of love, pleasure, and punishment await."

Epilogue – Jess

J ess parted the gauze curtains, taking in everything on the beach below her villa. Excitement made her eager to walk down the flower-petal-strewn aisle. The two years since Jasper asked her to marry him all over again passed in a whirlwind of love, life, and dirty diapers.

Their twins, Jade and Julia - yeah, they kept the J name tradition alive and well - arrived via c-section a month before their due date. They spent a week in the NICU, where neither she nor Jasper left their sides for more than a few minutes until they brought them home from the hospital.

Recovery took time, and Jasper helped with everything. When Jess returned to work, putting her nursing skills to use at Lavender House a couple of days a week while also pursuing her photography, they hired Tasha, their wonderful nanny, who now lived in the basement apartment of their brownstone.

On the twins' first birthday, Jasper asked if he could take care of the details of their vow renewal, and Jess agreed.

Best. Decision. Ever.

Her responsibility? Dress shopping with her friends to select the perfect gown for a beach wedding. Jasper kept her in the dark, convincing her they'd get married at a place in the Hamptons until they arrived at the airport and boarded a plane filled with all their friends and family headed to New Zealand.

They arrived five days ago at the resort Jasper rented out. Yup. The entire resort.

He arranged group tours, activities, and dinner every night in the restaurant dining room. Over mimosas this morning, Addie proclaimed Jasper's dedication to making this the perfect celebration was inspiring her next novel.

It's about an alpha billionaire who spoils the woman he's obsessed with while totally dicking her down. It sounded like Jess's next favorite read.

Addie, Joanna, and Kari left ten minutes ago, along with her mother, taking the twins down to the sandy beach to give Jess a few moments alone.

Jess spied the women making their way down the makeshift aisle. Kari held Jade, Addie kept a firm hold on a wiggling Julia, and Joanna carried a vocal Sara-Jane demanding to be put down to play in the sand, making Jess laugh when she heard Joanna negotiating with the three-year-old to not ruin her dress.

"Fuck, sweetheart. You take my breath away." Jessica gasped and spun away from the open patio door. Jasper's gaze raked over her from head to toe, searing her skin like he'd reached out and touched her.

He did an excellent job of taking her breath away, too, and never looked more handsome in his cream linen suit, leaving the first few buttons undone on the white shirt he wore beneath his jacket. Jasper even got his hair and beard trimmed and styled.

"My God, you're sexy, too." She shook her head and snatched the robe she'd left draped on the chair to cover her dress. "Wait. Never mind your sexy voodoo style. You're not supposed to see the bride until the ceremony."

"Don't deny me," Jasper said, tugging the robe from her grasp. The first time around, Jess opted for a soft and flowy maxi dress when they'd married in their backyard. This time, she chose something more elegant and fitting a beachy vibe.

Strapless with a corset bodice and a flowing silk skirt paired with strappy gold sandals. Jess kept the color warm cream to match her husband's suit, and the dress highlighted the tattoos on her arms and upper body.

The stylist Jasper hired smoothed her dark hair into a sleek ponytail, and the woman who did her makeup gave her smoky eyes and warm, peachy lips.

"Stunning." Jasper slipped his hands into his pockets and stepped closer, a look of intent desire upon his face. The late afternoon sun reflected on the gold chain he'd never removed hanging between the lapels of his shirt. Still carrying the rings, he planned to return to their rightful place through her healed nipple piercings in a private ceremony between them later tonight.

Jasper's heated smile grew wicked, and he cupped her face, careful not to mess with her makeup or hair. "Sweetheart, I fucked your sweet pussy a few hours ago. So, I'm sure we did away with tradition a while ago."

His intense gaze locked with hers. "I'm sorry I ruined your surprise. With how beautiful you are, there's no way I could keep my hands off you in front of everyone. I needed this moment. Just us."

"Jasper...." Jess raised up on her toes to bring her lips to his, but he held her still, a breath away from tasting him.

"I don't want to ruin your lipstick."

"You won't. Kiss me. Please." His warm breath skated over her parted lips, and Jess tried to taste the air he expelled with the tip of her tongue.

His mouth ghosted over hers. "If I kiss you, I'm going to need to make you come right fucking now."

"Yes, Jasper. Please fucking kiss me."

"As you wish." He knew what quoting one of her favorite movies did to her. His lips descended over hers in the lightest of kisses, making her moan with frustration when they parted all too soon.

"I didn't say which lips I planned to kiss." Then Jasper dropped to his knees and raised the skirt of her dress. His fingers traced up her calves, gathering the material in his hands until he held it at her hips.

Jess gasped when he pulled her lace panties to the side. "Fuck, you're soaked for me," he growled against her skin.

Jess moaned when he pressed an open-mouth kiss to her mound, tongue fucking her pussy, putting all his pent-up passion and desire into pleasuring and plundering between her slick folds. "Oh, yes...fuck yes, Jasper. Make me come."

She cupped the back of his head, and Jasper wrapped his arms around her waist, pulling her close. "I want the smell of your delicious cunt in my nose. I want to taste you on my lips while I repeat my vows. Come for me, wife. Come all over my tongue."

Jess hooked her right leg over Jasper's shoulder, holding him tight and rocking against his face. Her core tightened, fluttering and clenching on nothing while rippling waves of pleasure coursed through her body, and she came against his face, chanting his name over and over again.

Jasper licked and suckled her pussy, extending her orgasm until it became too much, and she needed to lower her trembling leg to the floor. He pulled her panties back into place and let the skirt of her dress fall back around her legs. Jasper caressed her cheek when he stood and asked, "Ready to marry me all over again, Jess?"

"So fucking ready." Jasper didn't let go, staring into her eyes. Then Jess heard one of their favorite songs' haunting yet beautiful opening notes. "Did you...?" Her words trailed off when she turned toward the sound.

"Go find out."

She stepped through the open patio door, and Jasper stood beside her when she looked toward the front of the gathered crowd. The lead singer of Death Cab for Cutie stood strumming a guitar to the side of the altar.

"How...?"

"I called in a favor, and he liked the idea of a little vacation. His wife's sitting in the back row and can't wait to meet you."

"They've been here this entire time?"

Jasper chuckled. "No, they flew in two days ago, and you almost spotted them four times."

"This is insane. I can't believe you did all this for me." This man loved her in ways she never imagined.

"Forever isn't enough time to show you how much I love you. Like the song says, Jess. I'll follow you into the dark."

Ben tipped his chin toward them, and their guests all turned in their direction at once. Jasper tucked her hand in the crook of his elbow, ready to walk down the aisle by her side. "Okay, Mrs. Jones?"

"Always and forever, Mr. Jones."

Thank You

Thank you for reading. If you enjoyed this book, please consider leaving a review on Amazon and/or Goodreads. Reviews help Indie Authors so much, and I appreciate every one of you. Happy Reading!

Also by K.C. Ford

Club Decadent Series

One Night at Club Decadent (prequel) (MF/FF/FFM/MFM/MMF Married Couple Polysexual Romance)

Their Protective Dom Bk 1(MMF Bodyguard Sword-Crossing Age-Gap Romance)

Addie & Gray Bk 2 (MF Older Woman/Younger Man Romance)

Jess & Jasper Bk 3 (MF Second-Chance Married Couple Romance)

Their Valentine Dom (novella) (MMF Holiday Smut-filled Romance)

Kari & West Bk 4 Coming Soon (MF Bi4Bi Age-Gap Romance)

Their Primal Dom (novella) (MMF Primal Play Lactation Kink Smut-Filled Romance) Coming Soon

One Weekend in Connecticut (novella) (MF/MMMF/MFM/MMF Married Couple Polysexual Romance) Coming Soon

Standalones – Wide Releases Available Everywhere

The Contract (novella) (MMF Married Couple Cuckhold Bi-Awakening Romance)

It Started with a Gym Crush (MF Older Woman/Younger Man Age-Gap Romance) Coming Soon

Follow Me

Follow my Amazon Author Page to get notified of my latest release.

K.C. Ford Author Page

Visit my website for First Chapter Previews, Content Warnings, and Bonus Chapters.

Author K.C. Ford Website

www.ingramcontent.com/pod-product-compliance
Lightning Source LLC
Chambersburg PA
CBHW030936260626
47169CB00002B/502